Emily Harvale lives i – although she wou French Alps ... or Can has several months of snow. Emily loves snow almost as much as she loves Christmas.

Having worked in the City (London) for several years, Emily returned to her home town of Hastings where she spends her days writing ... and wondering if it will ever snow.

You can contact her via her website, Facebook or Instagram.

There is also a Facebook group where fans can chat with Emily about her books, her writing day and life in general. Details can be found on Emily's website.

Author contacts:
www.emilyharvale.com
www.twitter.com/emilyharvale
www.facebook.com/emilyharvalewriter
www.instagram.com/emilyharvale

***

Scan the code above to see all Emily's books on Amazon

Also by this author

The Golf Widows' Club
Sailing Solo
Carole Singer's Christmas
Christmas Wishes
A Slippery Slope
The Perfect Christmas Plan
Be Mine
It Takes Two
Bells and Bows on Mistletoe Row

Lizzie Marshall series:
Highland Fling – book 1
Lizzie Marshall's Wedding – book 2

Goldebury Bay series:
Ninety Days of Summer – book 1
Ninety Steps to Summerhill – book 2
Ninety Days to Christmas – book 3

Hideaway Down series:
A Christmas Hideaway – book 1
Catch A Falling Star – book 2
Walking on Sunshine – book 3
Dancing in the Rain – book 4

Hall's Cross series
Deck the Halls – book 1
The Starlight Ball – book 2

Michaelmas Bay series
Christmas Secrets in Snowflake Cove – book 1
Blame it on the Moonlight – book 2

Lily Pond Lane series
The Cottage on Lily Pond Lane – four-part serial
Part One – New beginnings
Part Two – Summer secrets
Part Three – Autumn leaves

Part Four – Trick or treat
Christmas on Lily Pond Lane
Return to Lily Pond Lane
A Wedding on Lily Pond Lane
Secret Wishes and Summer Kisses on Lily Pond Lane

Wyntersleap series
Christmas at Wynter House – Book 1
New Beginnings at Wynter House – Book 2
A Wedding at Wynter House – Book 3
Love is in the Air – spin off

Merriment Bay series
Coming Home to Merriment Bay – Book 1
(four-part serial)
Part One – A Reunion
Part Two – Sparks Fly
Part Three – Christmas
Part Four – Starry Skies
Chasing Moonbeams in Merriment Bay – Book 2
Wedding Bells in Merriment Bay – Book 3

Seahorse Harbour series
Summer at my Sister's – book 1
Christmas at Aunt Elsie's – book 2
Just for Christmas – book 3
Tasty Treats at Seahorse Bites Café – book 4
Dreams and Schemes at The Seahorse Inn – book 5
Weddings and Reunions in Seahorse Harbour – book 6

Clementine Cove series
Christmas at Clementine Cove – book 1
Broken Hearts and Fresh Starts at Cove Café – book 2
Friendships Blossom in Clementine Cove – book 3

Norman Landing series
Saving Christmas – book 1
A not so secret Winter Wedding – book 2
Sunsets and surprises at Seascape Café-book 3
A Date at the end of The Pier – book 4

Locke Isle series

A Summer Escape – book 1

Christmas on Locke Isle – book 2

Betancourt Bay series

That Mistletoe Moment – book 1

That Winter Night – book 2

ISBN 978-1-909917-94-1

Published by Crescent Gate Publishing

Print edition published worldwide 2023
E-edition published worldwide 2023

Cover design by JR and Emily Harvale

Acknowledgements

My grateful thanks go to the following:

My webmaster, David Cleworth who does so much more than website stuff.
My cover design team, JR.
Luke Brabants. Luke is a talented artist and can be found at: www.lukebrabants.com
My wonderful friends for their friendship and love. You know I love you all.
All the fabulous members of my Readers' Club. You help and support me in so many ways and I am truly grateful for your ongoing friendship. I wouldn't be where I am today without you.
My Twitter and Facebook friends, and fans of my Facebook author page. It's great to chat with you. You help to keep me (relatively) sane!

To my friends, Ula and Grzesiek.
Thank you for helping my home look so festive.
Wishing you a very Merry Christmas!

Emily Harvale

Christmas on Locke Isle

CRESCENT GATE PUBLISHING

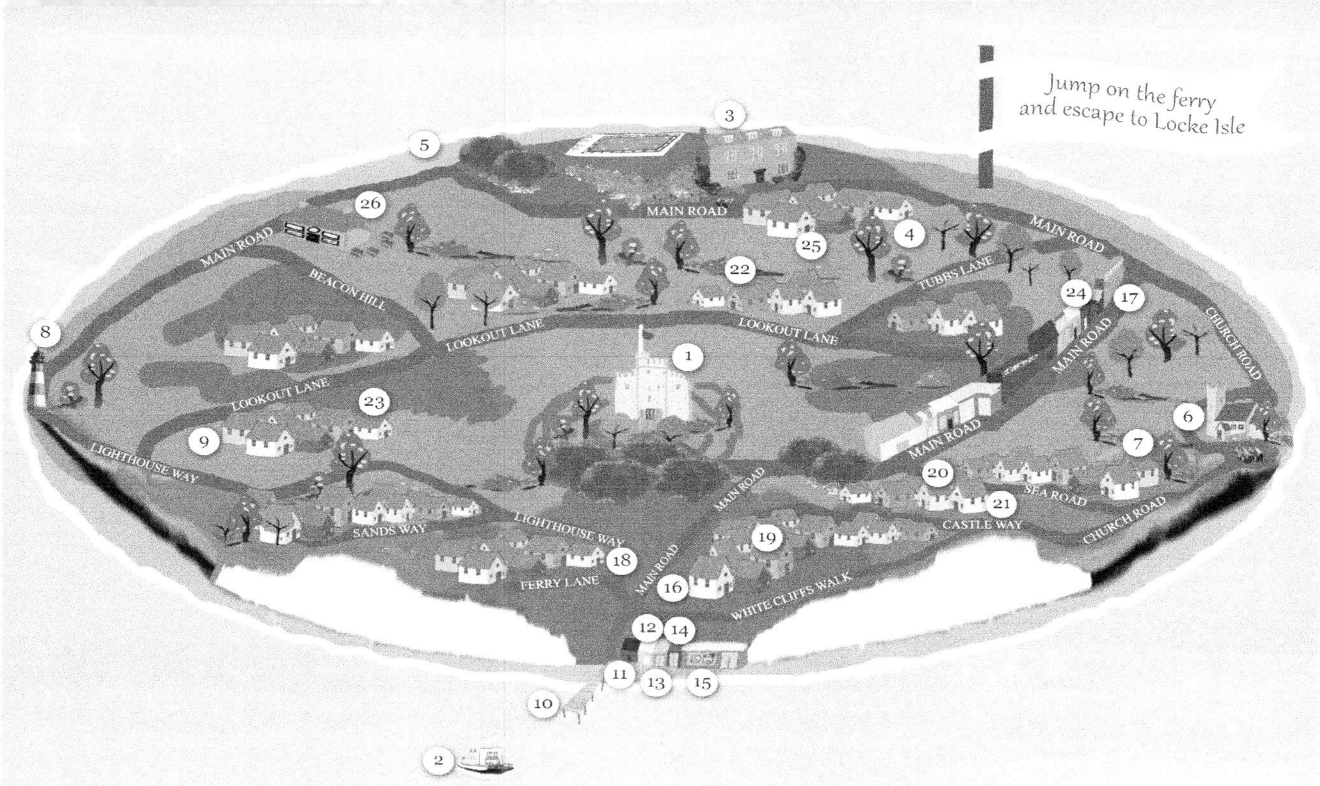

Jump on the ferry
and escape to Locke Isle
MAIN ROAD
MAIN ROAD
MAIN ROAD
MAIN ROAD
MAIN ROAD
MAIN ROAD
BEACON HILL
LOOKOUT LANE
LOOKOUT LANE
LOOKOUT LANE
TUBBS LANE
CHURCH ROAD
CHURCH ROAD
LIGHTHOUSE WAY
LIGHTHOUSE WAY
SANDS WAY
FERRY LANE
WHITE CLIFFS WALK
CASTLE WAY
SEA ROAD
1
2
3
4
5
6
7
8
9
10
11
12
13
14
15
16
17
18
19
20
21
22
23
24
25
26

MAP KEY – LOCKE ISLE

1. **Locke Keep** – The castle-like home of Ward Locke. His ancestors had owned Locke Isle and everything on it for centuries, but his grandfather and father have sold certain properties to the residents over the last hundred years.
2. **Locke Isle Ferry** – owned and operated by Ward Locke.
3. **Castle Keep Hotel** – luxury hotel (and former Mansion House home of Ward's Aunt Agatha) owned by Ward Locke but managed by Tristan Goldsby. The hotel is the place to go for the Spa and the heated pool.
4. **Frenchman's Cottage** - Tristan Goldsby, the manager of Castle Keep Hotel lives here
5. **Frenchman's Cove** – this is the beach adjoining the hotel.
6. **Church of St Mary on the Water** – The Reverend Minton Bloom is the vicar. He's in his 70s and hard of hearing but he's determined to remain in post.
7. **Land's End House** – the Rectory

8. **The Lighthouse** – it still functions and does an important job in keeping the heavy traffic in the English Channel away from the island and the rocks.
9. **Lookout Cottage** - this is where the lighthouse keeper, Jonas Barnaby lives with his wife Nell.
10. **Boardwalk** – part of this structure juts out to sea and it's where the ferry docks, and part is on dry land and is a promenade with a small parade of shops and a café.
11. **Locke Isle Tourist Office** – It's the first building you reach on Boardwalk, has a purple-painted façade ... and always seems to be closed.
12. **Duponts -** Frederick Dupont – Tailor, and his wife Esther Dupont – Dressmaker, work here but they live in the aptly named, Haberdasher's Cottage. The shop front is brightly painted, yellow and green.
13. **Buds and Blooms**, - is the florist shop, painted orange, and owned and run by Bernie (Bernadette) Burns, a widow for three years.
14. **White Cliffs Café** – is painted

blue. It is owned and run by two sisters, Sylvia (Sylvie) Shaw, the youngest, and Celia Thatcher (Cece) the eldest. They are both in their fifties, and single, although Cece is a widow. They also have an older brother, Alfred, who has been a widower for ten years but he's always had a soft spot for Bernie, the florist.

15. **Locke's Convenience Store** – owned by Ward's, Aunt Agatha (Aggie)
16. **White Cliffs Cottage** – home to Tracy (65) and Roger White (80) it's close to the cliff edge, although not as close as some of the other properties on the island. Roger was the ferryman all his life until he retired at 79 Tracy and Roger met on the ferry and they've been married for 20 years. Tracy was Geneva's nanny from the day of Geneva's birth until she was 8, when Tracy was sacked.
17. **The Clothing Locker** –It's owned by Agatha Locke, Ward's aunt, but Natalie Harte runs it.
18. **Bluebell Cottage** – Bernie Burns lives here
19. **Honeysuckle Cottage** – Alfred

Shaw lives here

20. **Magpie Cottage** – Cece Thatcher lives here
21. **Wren Cottage** – Sylvie Shaw lives here
22. **Haberdasher's Cottage** – home to Frederick Dupont and his wife Esther.
23. **Lockekeep Cottage** – home to Ward's aunt, Agatha Locke (Aggie)
24. **Fifi's Cuisine** – French restaurant on Main Road
25. **Croft Cottage** – Natalie Harte lives here with her young daughter, and her mum. The father of Natalie's child ran off and joined the Navy and hasn't been seen since. He lived in Folkestone. Natalie works in The Clothing Locker and her mum looks after the child.
26. **The Beacon Inn** – the only pub on the island (although there is a bar in Castle Keep Hotel) Owned by Ward Locke but licensed to Harry Flight, who lives here with his wife June, their son, Roman and their daughter, Alana.

Wish you were here?

This new series is set on Locke Isle, a fictional island two miles off the Kent coast, and also partly in the real town of Folkestone, but I have added a few fictional things/places/businesses in Folkestone – like the slipway where the Locke Isle Ferry docks, among others, so please forgive me for that!

In addition to this, my other new series, Betancourt Bay which links to this Locke Isle series, is also set in a fictional village a mile from Folkestone. I've, sort of, 'demolished' everything that currently occupies this space in real life, and 'built' Betancourt Bay there instead. Apologies for that, but it was a necessary evil in order for me to tell these stories.

So if you know Folkestone and the surrounding area, you may not entirely recognise it when you read these books...

With love,
Emily xx

One

It's only three weeks until Christmas and my list of things I need to get done and dusted before the Big Day is longer than Father Christmas' Naughty or Nice List. I thought I might be on the nice side of that one this year, but I'm beginning to get the feeling that more than a few of the residents of Locke Isle would stick me on the naughty side. I think several would cross me off their Christmas card list if they could, but as I'm living with Ward and his daughter, Eve, both of whom all the islanders adore, I might be lucky enough to see my name added to at least some of the cards Eve has told me she, her dad, and their black Labrador, Horatio, receive each year. It would be a bit grim if the dog gets his name on more cards than me. But then again, he is a rather delightful dog.

Everyone loves Ward, Eve, and Horatio – and not just because Ward owns Locke Isle ... or much of it. His ancestors owned the whole place once, and everything on it, but several decades ago, Ward's grandfather decided it was time the residents owned their own homes and businesses and began selling properties off to any of the islanders who wanted to buy their own place. Ward's father continued that process, and Ward has followed in both of their footsteps.

You might think that means Ward is rich. Sadly for him, that's not the case. Ward, like his father and grandfather before him, is a bit of a softie when it comes to the islanders. Those who wanted to buy, but couldn't afford to do so outright, have either been granted interest free payment plans, or given long leases at peppercorn rents. I couldn't believe that when I heard it. Ward is far too generous for his own good. But I suppose that's one of the reasons I love him so much.

When I arrived here, back in August, and Ward and I fell in love at first sight, a few people seemed to like me too. Even when I moved into Locke Keep to live with Ward and Eve within a matter of days. Those people said it was Destiny and wished us true happiness. Especially my former Nanny, Tracy, and her husband, Roger.

Others said I was nothing but a 'gold digger' – until they discovered the size of my bank balance and realised that if anyone was digging for gold in our relationship, it was Ward, not me. I could've bought this island ten times over and still had change.

When everyone realised that I was willing to spend a large chunk of my money on improving things on the island, several people warmed to me. They, along with Ward, listened to my ideas and nodded eagerly in approval.

But some people didn't trust me. Not that I blamed them. They'd heard, or read, about Geneva McBriar – the Geneva McBriar I was before I came to Locke Isle – and they were waiting for me to show my true colours and announce that McBriar Properties would be building one of the company's signature resorts on the island. No matter how many times I reassured them that I have left my dad's company and that no resort will ever be built here – at least not by me – they said, 'We'll see.'

A few of them continue to say it, and now, as we rush towards Christmas, it's not just the weather that's turned a little chilly. Even some of those who liked me, are beginning to question my plans.

I'm sad that they feel this way about me, but I can deal with that. I'm used to people hating me so this is nothing.

Thanks to my dad's property empire in which I had worked since leaving university, and some wise investments I've made over the years, I'm mega-rich. And thanks to his movie star good looks, together with my mum's, who happened to be a supermodel, I'm beautiful with a body to die for. That's not me being arrogant; that's a fact.

But those aren't the only reasons so many people over the years have disliked me. I'm the first to admit that, like my dad, I was a ruthless business woman before I came to Locke Isle, and like my mum, I was a petulant and rather selfish bitch. But the reason I came here was to change all that, and I think I've been doing pretty well, despite everything.

The one thing that does terrify me though, is that Ward seems to be 'cooling off' a little too. Or maybe I'm imagining that. There's been a lot going on lately and we haven't been spending quite as much time together as we did for the first two months.

He's still as passionate as he was on day one, when we're in bed together, and he still kisses me every day and tells me he loves me, but he used to say how happy he was that I came here, and how excited he was by our plans for the future of Locke Isle. Now he says he thinks I might be going too far, too fast with my 'so-called' improvements.

'The Boardwalk is called the Boardwalk for a reason,' he says, buttering a thick slice of freshly baked bread that he bought from White Cliffs Café on his early morning walk. Cece and Sylvie, the two sisters who run the café, make the best bread I've ever tasted, and I've tasted bread from some of the classiest bakeries on the planet. Ward buys a fresh loaf every day, and he, Eve and I have breakfast together each morning. It's one of the routines I've come to love. Although not so much this morning. 'It's made of wood,' he continues, without looking at me. 'Replacing it with millions of tonnes of concrete might not be such a good thing. The Concrete Walk doesn't have quite the same ring to it.'

I wait to see if he smiles and I'm disappointed when he doesn't. I pour orange juice into three glasses, put the carton back in the fridge, and place the glasses on the ancient oak kitchen table.

'Yes. But it can still be called the Boardwalk, and we can have it clad with wood if that'll make you happy. We need the concrete to shore up the cliffs and build a solid foundation for all the new shops and businesses to sit on. Plus, that wooden jetty could collapse at any moment. Have you seen the state of it lately? That freak storm last week did more damage than you seem to realise. Every time the ferry docks beside it, it creaks and groans a little more. And whenever a car drives down it, I'm waiting for it to fall into the sea. Think how wonderful it'll be to have a concrete pier. A smaller version of the Harbour Arm in Folkestone. And also how great it'll be to have a proper boat house where the water taxi and the ferry can be safely moored.'

The water taxi is a new addition and one thing that all the islanders agree was an excellent idea of mine. I bought it the day after I first slept with Ward, which was also the day he asked me to move in with him, just two days after I stepped onboard the ferry to Locke Isle. This was definitely a whirlwind romance.

The water taxi arrived a few days later and it's saved both time and money. If you forget the several hundred thousand pounds it cost me to purchase it, that is, and the extra cost for the 'rush' order. Ward doesn't know I paid extra for that and I'm not going to tell him now.

Instead of filling the ferry with diesel and spending several minutes manoeuvring the aged vessel into position, including extending the smaller of two metal gangways, and all for just one passenger on some trips, the rather elegant, mahogany motor launch can simply pull up alongside the wooden jetty and people can hop on and off. It has a small wheelhouse for the captain, an enclosed cabin in which ten people can sit on luxurious leather seats and admire the view through the windows, or, in good weather, enjoy the wind in their hair thanks to the fully retractable sunroof, and a further open deck at the rear, large enough to accommodate an additional six passengers. The ferry takes a good ten minutes to cover the two-mile crossing; the motor launch does it in less than half that time. As the only vehicles allowed on the island are those owned by the residents, or those given permission from Ward, only a few cars make the crossing per week, so the motor launch is a god send.

As is the new, ferry captain. I can't tell you how relieved I was when Ward finally agreed to hire him. For a while, I wasn't sure he would, especially when it transpired that I once dated the top candidate's older brother. But even Ward could see that Grady was the perfect choice. He, like his brother Adam, has skippered every type of boat imaginable, from the tiniest dingy, to motor launches, to mega yachts, and even a cruise ship, not to mention he's a former high-flying officer in the Royal Navy in which he served for twelve years.

'He's too highly qualified,' Ward argued. 'He'll be bored within a week.'

'He wants to write a book,' I pointed out. 'This is the perfect job for him to do that.

He'll have lots of free time, which is exactly what he wants. He's just turned down an eye-watering offer to captain a super yacht in Dubai because he wants to be based in the UK so that he can see more of his family, who live in Dover. And he can do this job with his eyes closed.'

'That's my point. Once winter sets in, he may decide that the warm waters of Dubai are preferable to the choppy, freezing waters of the English Channel, and that ferrying people and the occasional vehicle back and forth is tedious. Plus, I can't afford to pay him an eye-watering sum.'

'I can. Not that he wants one. He told me that he's happy with whatever you plan to pay because he knows it's not a full-time job and he knows what it entails. Just like Roger, he simply wants to do something that'll keep him on the water.'

Ward finally conceded that it was worth giving Grady a shot and I think everyone is pleased with the way things have turned out.

Roger was the former ferry captain until he was too old to do the job, and Ward took over on a temporary basis. Roger had held the position for many years having been employed by Ward's dad, who was also a friend of Roger's. He eventually retired at seventy-nine, but he still went out with Ward from time to time, and he now does the same with Grady, who doesn't seem to mind.

Come to think of it, it was around the time that Grady took over as captain that Ward began behaving a little differently towards me. Or maybe I'm imagining that. He did ask a lot of questions about Grady's brother, Adam, the one I dated, and whether the man was likely to visit if Grady got the job. I told him it was unlikely because Adam did prefer warmer climes. That was one of the reasons we split up. Edinburgh was far too cold for Adam. And apparently, so was I, although I didn't tell Ward that bit.

Perhaps Ward misses being ferry captain. I know his daughter does. Eve's single ambition in life, so far at the age of eight, is to be a pirate captain. The day we met she told me she was the captain and the ferry was really a pirate ship. She goes to school in Folkestone, so she still crosses back and forth every day, weather permitting, but at first she said the journey wasn't the same as it was on the 'pirate ship'. Ward told her that all pirate captains had smaller boats to get to and from their ships and the motor launch is merely one of those, so that made her happy again.

Now Ward sighs and shakes his head as he passes me the jar of marmalade, along with the slice of bread he's buttered for me. Surely he must still truly love me if he butters my bread every day?

'I agree the jetty does seem a little more rickety lately and I'm all for shoring it up, but does it have to be all concrete? A pier would be nice, but it'll take months to build. And yes, having somewhere to keep the water taxi and the ferry safe during the storms is a wonderful idea. I'm simply wondering if this 'boat house' needs to be the size of an aircraft hangar? Are you planning to build a runway along the beach too, and parking your company jet? And will there soon be a McBriar Airlines flying to and from the island?'

He meets my eye and as I can see there's a hint of concern in his, I decide that this might not be the best time to mention that I have been considering the possibility of having a helipad added somewhere.

I smile lovingly and pour us both coffee from the fresh pot on the table.

'Firstly, if that did happen – and I'm not suggesting for one moment that it should, it would be called Locke Airlines, not McBriar. And secondly, I don't have a company jet. That belongs to my dad. Well, to McBriar Properties as far as the tax office is concerned.' I grin at him but Ward just shakes his head. 'I thought you wanted all this, Ward. I thought you'd agreed the plans. But if you're saying you've changed your mind, or that there's something that needs tweaking, that's fine. Just tell me what you want instead.'

He holds my gaze for a moment before letting out another small sigh. 'I do want it, Gen. I do. But I also want things to be like they were. And we'd all like some peace and quiet again, especially as it's getting close to Christmas. Having massive cranes, lorries, portacabins, building materials, and about fifty men on the beach for the last month hasn't been exactly ideal, has it? This island was idyllic, now it's just a building site.'

I can't argue with that. Locke Keep sits on a large mound in the centre of the island and its walls are at least fifteen inches thick yet we can still hear the noise from the site that was once a blissfully peaceful, sandy beach. I can only imagine what it must sound like from the inside of one of the cottages sitting on the cliffs right above it.

Actually, I don't have to imagine that. I was having afternoon tea at Tracy's cottage the other day, which is fairly close to, but not directly above the site. We almost had to shout at one another to be heard over the din. And the cups did a little dance in their saucers every time the drilling started up again.

Concrete piles are going into the shore to support the new extension to the

'Boardwalk'. The current wooden one runs along the base of the cliffs on one side of the road down to the beach and forms a promenade on which White Cliffs Café sits, together with Locke's Convenience Store, owned by Ward's aunt, the florists Buds and Blooms, Duponts tailors and dressmakers, and Locke Isle Tourist Office. From there it meets the road and then juts out to sea to form the jetty at which the ferry and the water taxi dock. I suggested extending the Boardwalk to the other side of the road, where more shops could be situated, both for the benefit of the islanders and for tourists.

Plus concrete supports are going in to shore up the crumbling cliffs to ensure the cottages sitting far too close to the edge for comfort, won't topple over the cliff and crash onto the beach a hundred or so feet below.

Ward, and most of the islanders, especially those living in the endangered cottages, loved the idea, but when work commenced, once the main tourist season ended in late October, and the reality of what was involved became clear, there were a few dissenting voices. They seem to have grown louder during November, especially when people saw the dimensions of the boat house which will be situated at the end of the new extension.

I've been thinking that a helipad could

be added further along the beach, near the lighthouse, perhaps. Or better yet, close to Castle Keep Hotel, the luxury, former Mansion House, hotel on the other side of the island. It's owned by Ward but managed by a rather dashing man called Tristan Goldsby. But I won't mention the helipad just yet.

'I know,' I say. 'And I'm sorry about that, but Cece and Sylvie aren't complaining, and nor are most of the shop and business owners, including your own aunt. Those fifty men – some of which are women, by the way, have been spending rather a lot of money on this island. You said yourself that the hotel, shops, café, restaurant, pub and its B&B, are full for the first time in years. Okay, it's with the workforce rather than holidaymakers, but nevertheless, it's still income. And you also said that hardly anyone visits the island in November, so although the building work may be noisy and messy and disruptive, it'll all be worth it when it's done.'

'Will it?'

'Yes. Trust me, Ward. I've been involved with hundreds of sites just like this one and the first month is always the hardest.' That's only a small lie, and hopefully he won't remember it once he sees the final results.

'Really?' He looks doubtful as I pass the marmalade back to him.

'Uh-huh.' I finally sit down at the table as Eve and Horatio tumble into the kitchen to join us. And I do mean tumble.

'Please don't play-fight with Horatio in the kitchen,' Ward says, although now he is grinning. 'And wash your hands before you sit at the table.'

'Morning!' Eve sings out as she dashes to the sink. Horatio barks and chases after her.

As it's Saturday, she's in full pirate mode and dressed in black and white striped trousers, black trainers, and a black T-shirt emblazoned with a large skull and crossbones with bright red flashing eyes. I bought her the T-shirt and, not only do the eyes flash, if you press its jaw it says, 'Shiver me timbers, Matey. I'll slit your throat, if you don't walk that plank.' I'm not sure everyone was delighted with my choice, apart from Eve.

'Morning gorgeous,' I say, and when Eve beams at me I add, 'I was talking to the dog.'

She giggles, and as she does every morning now, she comes and gives me a massive hug and plants a small kiss on my cheek.

The first time she did it, I was surprised, and so was Ward. 'She really loves you, Gen,' he said, and although he seemed genuinely pleased about that, I think he was also a little concerned.

Eve's mum died when Eve was only two, so Ward's aunt, Agatha, and my former Nanny, Tracy have been the motherly figures in her life. And then I appeared on the scene and moved in with Ward and her, and since then, well, she seems to see me as one of the family. I think I rank equally with Horatio in Eve's affections. High praise indeed. And I'm not even being sarcastic.

Until I came here, kids hadn't really featured in my life. I assumed I might have one if I married, but to me they were more of a possession; something a person had, along with the house, the car, the pool, the pedigree dog. That's how I had been brought up. Yet the moment I met Eve, I think I fell in love.

Ward sometimes jokes that I fell for Eve first and then for him, and there may be some truth in that.

It really was the strangest feeling. From almost the second she took my hand I felt that there was something special between us. Some sort of inexplicable bond.

I felt something for Ward the moment I met him too, but it was a completely different feeling. And not so inexplicable.

Ward was handsome, sexy as hell, fit and strong. Eve was ... simply Eve.

In the months that have passed, I've grown to love both Ward and Eve even more than I did when I met them. Eve feels the same way about me, I'm sure of that. Ward, as I said, did too, but perhaps not so much right now.

Having 'lost' the last man I thought I was in love with to someone else, the thought of losing Ward genuinely terrifies me. So much so, I can't bear to think about it. I never felt for Mack the things I feel for Ward. I thought my heart was broken when Mack dumped me. I honestly think I might die if Ward does the same.

'So what's the plan for today then?' Ward asks, smiling at Eve as she takes her seat at the table, and then at me as Horatio curls up on my feet, close to Eve but far enough away that he doesn't get kicked in the head by her swinging legs and feet.

'I've got to get some things ticked off my list,' I say, between gulps of coffee.

'We can help,' says Eve, meaning her and Horatio, not Ward.

'Well,' says Ward. 'Looks like I've got a free day then.'

'In your dreams,' I say, raising my eyebrows for added effect as he leisurely sips his orange juice. 'Just because you're no longer ferry captain, it doesn't mean you can lounge around all day.' I tut and then laugh. 'There're only three weeks till Christmas, and we need to get a move on if this is to be the best one yet.'

A furrow forms between his brows. 'Er … why does this one have to be the best one yet? And what, exactly, are you planning, Gen? I assumed you meant your list for the ongoing building work, not a list for Christmas.'

'Ah. Did I not mention it before? I was sure I had.'

He slowly shakes his head. 'No, Gen. You did not.'

'Oooh!' shrieks Eve. 'What are you planning?' She sounds far more enthusiastic than her dad.

'Lots and lots of lovely festive surprises,' I say, tapping my nose. 'You'll have to wait and see.'

I don't need to look at Ward to know he's rolling his eyes, but I can hear the sigh that goes with it.

I genuinely thought I had mentioned my plans for Christmas to him, but obviously not. The problem is, we've both been so busy – me, with the work to the Boardwalk; Ward, with finding the new captain for the ferry, and then catching up with all the other things he does in relation to keeping the ferry afloat and all the many businesses on the island, in which he has a stake or an interest – that we don't seem to have much time to sit and talk since the building work began at the end of October.

Or perhaps it is partly because he gave

me a bit of a lecture over the amount of money I spent making Halloween special for everyone on the island this year. And another small lecture when I made sure our bonfire was big enough to be seen from the mainland on Guy Fawkes Night.

'You don't have to keep spending money to make people like you, Gen,' he said, as the parade of professional actors, dancers and jugglers made their way down Main Road on Halloween, and the chocolate fountains overflowed, and metal balls containing bags of sweets shot out from specially made cannons in front of Locke Keep.

'I'm not trying to make people like me,' I said. 'I'm trying to make everyone as happy as you and Eve have made me.'

He kissed me passionately then even though he wasn't entirely convinced about my motives, but that was the honest truth.

I will admit that, perhaps, the bonfire on the beach on Guy Fawkes Night was a bit too big, and possibly also the actual Guy. The pile of wood was almost as high as the cliffs and when the wind suddenly picked up and blew flames and several large sparks, along with a burning arm from the Guy, towards some of the cottages, and the businesses on the wooden Boardwalk, even I was concerned.

Luckily the workmen and women from the building site had a ready supply of hoses and water, so there were no serious issues. There is a fire truck, along with two volunteer firefighters on the island, but they weren't needed, thankfully.

And all the islanders loved the food and beverages I'd supplied, and the fireworks went down a treat, especially as they were the silent type. Although one or two did cause a tiny bit of damage to a couple of the gardens when they burnt themselves out. I paid for the plants to be replaced, and most people seemed to have fun.

But maybe I subconsciously avoided discussing Christmas in case I got another lecture.

I'm making Ward sound as if he's a bit of a grinch, but he isn't. He's kind and caring, loving and supportive, generous to a fault, and as hot as hell. He's also fun and has a great sense of humour. I think it's me who is the one with the problem.

Having worked for Dad's company, McBriar Properties, for most of my adult life, I've been used to making decisions on my own, and on the spur of the moment. I only needed to run things by Dad if I had any doubts – which was rare, or if a deal was going to cost us more than we'd anticipated. Having to discuss things with someone else is a fairly new concept for me. Even when I dated Mack, who also worked for the company, I was the boss and Mack basically did what I told him to. Until he fell in love with another woman.

It's a completely different situation with Ward. I have to remind myself that this is his island, not mine, and that he's the one who should be making decisions, not me.

'I think we need to discuss this list of yours,' Ward says.

And I brace myself for another one of his little lectures about me not spending all my money. As if I ever could. I still don't think he's entirely grasped the fact that I'm a multi-millionaire.

Or perhaps he simply doesn't want to remind himself of that.

When the work began on the Boardwalk, Ward told me he was in awe of my knowledge and my business acumen. He stood by my side as I held my own with all the experts I'd brought in. He listened avidly as we went over the plans, dimensions, materials, potential problems, workforce requirements, and timing. On one or two occasions I forgot he was there and had to remind him that he should feel free to add input whenever he wanted, but other than asking for clarification about a couple of things, he really left it all to me.

'This is how you and your dad made your millions,' he said, when I asked if everything was okay. 'Far be it from me to pretend I know better than you and the other experts. And it is your money you are spending, not mine.'

'Is something wrong, Ward?' I had asked. 'Because if you're unhappy about any of this you only have to say and I'll do whatever you want or need.'

'No,' he said, pulling me into his arms and kissing me. 'It's just ... me being an idiot, that's all. Watching you over the last few days has made me feel ... well ... a little emasculated, I suppose. You're the one with all the money, the one with the power, the knowledge, the expertise. I want to be the one who provides for you. The one who makes you feel proud.'

'Oh, Ward,' I said, before he could continue. 'You do provide for me. You've provided me with a wonderful, loving homelife. One I never thought I would have. I've been happier here with you, Eve, and Horatio than I ever dreamt I could be. And you own an island! As for making me feel proud, I feel that every time I look at you. You have knowledge and expertise I could never hope to have. You're adored by everyone on this island and I'm so proud to be your girlfriend. And as for power, you have the power to turn me to mush with just a look, to melt me with just a smile, and the power to make my heart soar, or to break it if you stop loving me.'

'Stop loving you? That'll never happen, Gen,' he said.

And when he kissed me again, I believed him.

So why do I now feel that he might?

Two

'Reindeer!' Ward's brows knit together and his mouth stays open as he stares at my Christmas list via the screen of my iPad.

That's only number one on the list, although I did tell him that it's not in order of priority and that I merely noted items down as they popped into my head, but judging by his astonishment, we're not off to the best start.

Eve and Horatio are playing in her room because I didn't want to spoil the surprise for her, but I didn't expect Ward to be the one who is surprised.

'You don't mean *real* reindeer?' He raises his eyes to mine and shakes his head. 'Do you?'

I smile sheepishly and nod. 'They need to be real to pull Santa's sleigh.'

'Santa's sleigh?' The high-pitched tone at the end of that can't be good.

'Number six on the list,' I say.

He stares at the screen and gulps. 'Ah yes. I see. After Elves, A barn, Father Christmas, and Reindeer food.' He looks at me. 'A barn?'

'For the Reindeer.'

The snort of laughter does not bode well. 'Of course. Silly me. Wait! What? Polar bears! You have got to be kidding!'

'Not real ones. Polar bears can be dangerous. I've seen them in their natural habitat, so I know. You can buy life-sized ones that look real though. I thought a family of three would be good.'

He stares at me in silence and then returns to my list.

'Penguins?'

'They will be real. They'll look so cute in a pool with fake icebergs.' I beam with excitement. 'I love penguins and I know Eve will be thrilled. I thought the fake polar bears could be on top of the icebergs but then it dawned on me that the penguins might not realise the bears were fake and they might get freaked out.'

'Uh-huh,' he says. 'And we wouldn't want that, would we? Are you completely mad, Gen?' His expression tells me he thinks I am. 'Forgetting, for one moment, that we don't have a pool – unless you're suggesting we use the one at Castle Keep Hotel ... and I truly hope *you are not*, because that is a definite NO!'

'No,' I say. 'I was planning on having a temporary one built.'

'Of course you were.' He frowns deeply before continuing. 'Where was I? Oh yes. And we don't have fake icebergs, or polar bears, nor real penguins, or reindeer – and you said yourself that it's only three weeks until Christmas, how and when are you planning to get all these things here? And who, exactly, is going to look after the real reindeer and real penguins?'

'The Elves, of course.'

His brows shoot sky-high. And then he tuts. 'What is wrong with me? Elves are the obvious choice. G-E-N!' The way he drags out my name tells me he's not entirely on board with my ideas.

'I realise I've left it a bit late, but with all the building work, and everything else going on, I hadn't got around to writing a list until yesterday. The Elves will be trained professionals in animal care and management. They'll dress as Elves so that they fit in with all the rest of the Elves who'll be working in Santa's village.'

Colour drains from his cheeks. 'Santa's ... village?'

'Number twenty-five,' I say. 'You'll see it when you scroll down. It's going to be near the pool I'll have built ... and the ice rink.'

'Pool *AND* Ice rink? Seriously?'

I clear my throat. 'Numbers twenty-eight and twenty-nine on the list.'

He blinks several times and returns his attention to my iPad screen.

'Three giant Christmas trees. Must be at least thirty feet.' He sucks in a breath. 'Three thirty-foot trees? Dare I ask where you plan to put those?'

'I realise that should be four. I'll change that. One will go near the lighthouse, one at the other end of the island, beside the church, one will go outside here, at the foot of the steps, perhaps? And the fourth one will be for the Great Hall. Although ... do you think we should also have one somewhere on Main Road?'

'Oh, absolutely.' His tone, however, suggests the opposite.

'And ... perhaps one for the ferry?' I add, hesitantly.

'Surely that goes without saying?' he says with a shaky laugh. 'And we must have one stuck on the front of the water taxi too, don't you think? Although not one of thirty feet. That might sink the boat. Is drowning by Christmas tree a thing, I wonder?'

'You're making fun of me, aren't you?' I can't help but feel a little hurt.

He looks me in the eye, lets out a long sigh, puts my iPad down on the kitchen table and after another shake of his head, leans forward and takes my hands in his.

'I'm sorry, Gen. I didn't mean to. But are you serious? Don't you think you might be overdoing things just a tad? How long is that list, by the way?' He nods towards the discarded iPad.

'Fifty-five items,' I say tentatively, lowering my gaze and my head. 'But it's not finished. And I'm counting things like the Elves, and the penguins, as one item each, even though there will be lots of them.'

His sharp intake of breath is audible but he coughs to try to cover it up.

'Gen?' Now his voice is soft and low and actually rather sexy. 'Christmas is not about spending a fortune. It's not about reindeer, or penguins, or polar bears, or pools, or ice rinks, or Santa's village ... or Elves. It's about spending time with people you care about. It's about decorating a tree. One tree. And preferably smaller than thirty feet. It's about carol singing around the island. Having snowball fights and building snowmen – weather permitting. Wait. Did I see snow on your list?'

I raise my eyes to his and nod. 'And a snow machine to make it. And a ski slope. Just a small one. Numbers nineteen to twenty-one.'

He closes his eyes and screws up his nose

for just a moment.

'You're not happy, are you?' I ask.

He slowly shakes his head. 'This isn't about me being happy, Gen. Tell me something. What do you and your family usually do at Christmas? Do you have all the things on that list?'

'Sometimes,' I say. 'Sort of. We often go to the family ski chalet, in Aspen, Colorado. But not usually together. Dad only takes a couple of days off and then he's back at his desk. Mum pops in and out, depending how her mood takes her, and then jets off to warmer climes. Last year, Mack and … my ex and I went to stay with some people I know in Gstaad, Switzerland for a few days. But one year I went to Norway, and I did see polar bears. And one year, to Antarctica for Christmas and New Year. I saw penguins, and some penguin chicks being born, which was magical. Oh, and humpback whales.' I let out a wistful sigh as I remember that holiday.

'Please don't tell me there's a humpback whale – or a whale of any kind – on your list.'

'Of course not,' I laugh. 'That would be ridiculous.'

He quirks a brow. 'Yet reindeer and penguins aren't?'

'No!' I meet his look and sigh. 'Okay. Perhaps I'm going a little over the top. But I want this Christmas to be special, Ward, that's all. It's my first Christmas here. My first Christmas as part of a real family. I mean, a family who wants to be together. I want to share as much fun and as many festivities with you, and Eve, and Horatio, and Aggie, as possible. And with friends. Like Tracy and Roger. And Natalie.'

'But you don't need reindeer and penguins to do that, Gen.'

'Maybe not. But I bet if you asked Eve if she'd like reindeer and penguins, and all the other stuff on my list, she'd say yes.'

'I'm sure she would. And if you asked her if she'd like a pirate ship, she'd say…' He stops and looks questioningly at me. 'There's a pirate ship on that list, isn't there?'

I shrug nonchalantly. 'Just a little one. And it's really a small sail boat made to look like a pirate ship. She loves boats so much that I thought…' Ward doesn't look happy. 'I … I ordered that back in late September. It's arriving on Christmas Eve.'

'And you didn't think that, perhaps, you should discuss that with me? Her dad?'

He's cross.

'It's going to be from both of us, Ward. Not just from me.'

'That's not the problem!' he snaps. 'She's eight, Gen.'

'It's perfect for someone of her age to learn to sail, Ward.' I'm getting a bit cross myself.

'Eve is my daughter. I should be the one to decide when she should learn to sail.'

Ah. Now I see his point.

Damn. I should've thought of that.

He's right.

'I'm so sorry, Ward. I … I didn't think it through. I thought she'd be excited. I thought you would too, in a way. It's … it's large enough to accommodate at least three people. I wasn't intending for her to go out on her own. I thought … hoped … we could all go out together. Horatio, too. But I can see what you're saying now. And yes. I should've asked. I'm sorry. I can … I can cancel it. Or give it to charity, I suppose.'

'Oh, Gen,' he says on a sigh. 'What am I going to do with you?'

'Forgive me?' I squeak, terrified he won't.

He shakes his head and a slow grin forms on his gorgeous mouth. He leans forward and kisses me on my forehead.

'There's nothing to forgive. I know you mean well. But next time you think of buying something for Eve, perhaps you'll run it by me first?'

'Definitely,' I say puffing out my bated breath. 'I promise.'

He looks me in the eye. 'It's arriving on Christmas Eve?'

'Uh-huh. Unless I tell them not to deliver it here.'

'And it's a real sail boat? A dinghy or small sailing yacht? It's safe and sound and sturdily built? It complies with all the safety rules and regs?'

'Absolutely! I would never buy anything that wasn't completely safe for her. And it comes with life jackets, flares, and ... well, it's utterly safe, so let's not worry about that.'

'Okay,' he laughs. 'And thank you. It's a wonderful present and Eve will be thrilled.'

'I hope so. But it's definitely from both of us, and I mean that.'

'Thank you. Erm...' A mischievous smile appears on his lips, and his eyes dance with amusement as he pulls me close. 'Is there anything for me on that list of yours?'

I beam at him as tingles shoot through me as they always do when he looks at me like that.

'I wouldn't have shown it to you if there was. I've got another list for presents. The pirate ship is on that one because I need to find somewhere for us to put it until Christmas Day. The boat house won't be ready in time, I don't think.'

'Another list?' He raises his brows. 'Not as long as that one, I hope.'

'You'll have to wait and see.'

Now he's serious again. 'Please don't

spend a fortune, Gen. I don't need expensive presents. There's nothing I want. Apart from you, that is. And you know that, with everything else I need to deal with on the island, I don't have lots of cash to spare for gifts. Can we just agree to buy each other something small, but meaningful this year? I don't want to come across as a grinch but–'

'There's no need to explain. And of course. I understand completely. I think that's a fantastic idea.' I grin at him. 'So only one pair of Christmas socks then and not the forty pairs I'd planned to buy?'

He laughs at that. 'With reindeers on them, preferably.'

And then he kisses me, and everything is right with the world.

At least for today.

Three

'Ward told me about your Christmas list,' Aggie, Ward's aunt says when I pop into Locke's Convenience Stores the following day.

'Oh? Well I think it needs some tweaking, so nothing's finalised yet.'

I'm trying to behave as if it's not a big deal, but I wish he hadn't told her. I'm still not convinced Aggie likes me, although Ward assures me, she does. Yet every time I see her, she looks at me as if I'm from another planet and she's not quite sure I'm human.

To be fair, we didn't really get off to a good start when we first met, back in August. I completely misunderstood our conversation, and then I climbed a tree in her garden – at Eve's request – and got a lecture about it from Ward.

Since then she's been friendly enough – apart from the looks she gives me. We even meet for coffee once a week in White Cliffs

Café. I try to make sure Tracy is with us as often as possible. In addition to being my former Nanny, and now a good friend, Tracy is a close friend of Aggie's and having her join us takes some of the pressure off me.

I still find it hard to believe that, for someone who was a ruthless business woman who could – and still can – handle herself in any business situation and negotiation, no matter how difficult or complicated, the thought of spending time alone with Aggie, fills my stomach with butterflies. And not in a good way.

What is really strange is that she doesn't even look intimidating. Far from it, in fact. She dresses like a former hippy. The day we met, she was wearing a long, floral-patterned skirt, a white blouse, and had bare feet. She's wearing similar clothes today, but has well-worn UGG ankle boots on her feet. She has the same wavy curls as Ward and Eve, but her long hair always seems to be tied loosely in a knot. She's tall, slim and attractive, and I originally assumed she was in her late fifties. I was amazed when Ward told me she is actually seventy-one. She doesn't have a single grey hair that I can see. I suppose she must colour it. I hope I look as good as she does when I'm in my seventies.

'I can see why you want to go all out this Christmas,' she says, 'but has it ever occurred to you that sometimes less is more?'

'No,' I say, being totally honest.

She quirks a brow and instantly reminds me of Ward.

'Hmm. Well sometimes it is. Take my word for that. Don't you have enough on your plate with all the building work? Surely restoring some peace and tranquillity to the island is far more important than shipping in a bunch of live creatures? And think of the progress the workforce could make if they continue building the Boardwalk rather than a pool for some penguins, and an ice rink for, I assume, the islanders.'

'I was intending to bring in an additional team to build the pool, ice rink, barn ... and Santa's village.'

'Ah yes. Santa's village. It's a lovely idea, Geneva, but have you actually counted how few young children there are on the island? Wouldn't your money be better spent taking the children, and their parents, into Folkestone to meet Father Christmas? They could spend the entire day there, have lunch, go ice skating, see the pantomime, visit the Christmas Market, and so much more, and you'd still only spend about a tenth of the cost of bringing all those things here. And you could even hire that additional team you mentioned, but to add to the workforce for the Boardwalk, meaning that would be finished sooner rather than later. But of course, you're the one with all the money to throw around, not me, and certainly not Ward, so it's your choice how you spend it. Just something to think about when you tweak that list. Now what did you come in for, my dear? I'm sure it wasn't to listen to me banging on, was it?'

I'm so disheartened by the time she's finished that I can't remember what I did come in for, but I'm not about to tell her that.

'Christmas Crackers,' I say, spotting several boxes of them piled high on a nearby shelf.

'Christmas Crackers? Really? I would've thought you'd be having those shipped in from Harrods or somewhere.'

'Fortnum & Mason. Have you seen their Regal Crackers? They're so pretty. And a mere one thousand pounds for a set of six. But I thought I'd see what you had. Do you sell luxury crackers, by any chance?'

She grins at me as if she thinks I'm joking, and she only gave a quick quirk of her brow when I mentioned the price. 'Not yet. But I'll be sure to order some for next year. Assuming you're still here.'

'Still here?' That took me by surprise. And it's knocked the wind out of my sails. Did Ward tell her more than just about the contents of my Christmas list? Has he ... has he told her he no longer feels the way he did when he asked me to move in? It was a whirlwind romance, as I said. And I've never been lucky in love. Those butterflies are gnawing at my insides 'Are you suggesting I might not be?' I can hear the shrill note of panic in my voice.

She shrugs. 'I don't know, Geneva. You tell me. I sincerely hope so.'

I don't understand. She actually sounds sincere.

'Do you? Only, I can't shake the feeling that I'm not really your cup of tea.'

'Oh? I don't know why you feel that. I thought I'd made it clear that I admire you and what you've achieved. My only slight concern is whether you're really here just for Ward and Eve, or whether your father figures somewhere in the equation. I know you've said that you've left his company and you won't be going back, but Ward and Eve mean the world to me and I don't want to see either of them hurt.'

I can't stop the gasp from escaping.

'They mean the world to me too, Aggie. And I have no intention of hurting them. Ever. As for my dad, I've made it clear to him that my life is here now. With Ward and Eve. It's true that he doesn't entirely believe me, but once he sees for himself how happy I am and how much I love them both, he'll realise

I mean what I say. If anyone ends up getting hurt here, it'll be me.'

'You? Why do you say that?'

'Because ... because you're right about that bloody Christmas list! And the noise and mess from the building work. All I want to do is improve things for everyone on the island. To do something nice. To help Ward in any way I can. And yet I don't seem to be able to get things right. I'm trying so hard to be a good person but I can't change the habits of a lifetime in a few short months, no matter how much I want to.'

To my surprise, she reaches out and squeezes my arm, and then she smiles. 'As I said at the start of this conversation, Geneva, sometimes less is more. You seem to think I don't like you, but you're wrong. I'm just concerned that you'll grow bored with the island and want to return to your jet set lifestyle. Ward and Eve adore you, and if you leave, it'll break their hearts. But if you really do love them – and I believe you do – all you need to do is show them that. Not by spending money all the time, but simply by being with them. Which you do. Surely you can see that it's those times when both Ward and Eve are happiest? It's not your money they love, Geneva. It's you. Me, on the other hand,' she grins. 'I rather like your money. You simply need to learn to spend it more wisely.'

I meet her look and suddenly wonder why I see her as a threat. She's simply looking out for Ward and Eve. Perhaps I should let my guard down with her more often and see if we could be friends.

'So ... the reindeer, penguins and all the rest, needs to be crossed off the list then? Is that what you're saying?'

'I haven't seen the list so I can't be sure, but from what Ward has told me I would say quite a lot of it needs to go. Yes. If you want to, why don't you, Ward and I meet for afternoon tea at my cottage later to discuss it? Unless you have other plans for today?'

'Only cancelling a few orders I placed yesterday,' I say with a determined grin. 'I don't think Ward's busy. He said he was having the day off. Afternoon tea sounds perfect. I truly appreciate any assistance you can give me, and I know Ward will welcome it. Wait. He didn't ask you to have a word with me about it, did he?'

She raises her brows. 'You're not a very trusting woman, are you, Geneva McBriar?' She smiles and shakes her head. 'No. I can promise you, he did not. This is my idea. But I do think we can all benefit from a chat about what we want this Christmas to be. A simple, homely Christmas like the one we've had each year, or an extravaganza of animals,

Elves, and heaven knows what. Or perhaps a combination of both. Let's meet at 3 p.m. and I'll ask Tracy to look after Eve. We don't want her getting as much as a whisper that reindeers might arrive on Locke Isle. Now what did you really come in to buy? Because I think we both know that it wasn't Christmas Crackers, was it?'

Four

How could I have been so wrong about Aggie? Am I also wrong about Ward? Perhaps he's not cooling towards me at all. Maybe it's just my fear of losing him that's making me see things that aren't there. Aggie said he adores me, and she would know how he feels. Ward and his aunt are extremely close.

I walk back up Main Road but instead of returning home, I veer off to the right.

"Home". I still get a warm glow deep inside me whenever I call Locke Keep my home. I've lived in Edinburgh for most of my life and yet neither McBriar House, the former stately home my dad owns and where I lived when I wasn't away at school, or my own apartment where I've lived for several years until I came here, feel like home now.

The moment I stepped inside Locke Keep it felt as if I'd come home. That was pretty weird because most people would say it's a draughty, crumbling, ancient fortress, not a cosy place to live. They'd be wrong. Yes it's an ancient fortress, and yes it's draughty at times, and it's definitely crumbling. But the first floor, which is where we live, feels like a comfortable, spacious apartment. Once the doors are closed and the fires are crackling in the gigantic hearths, and the heating is turned on, it's exceedingly cosy. It's a wonderful, magical place to live.

Ward has finally agreed to let me fund the repairs and restoration costs. At first he said no to that. He was willing to let me spend money on the Boardwalk because he believes that will ultimately benefit everyone on the island, but Locke Keep is his ancestral home and he said it wasn't right for me to spend hundreds of thousands of pounds on it.

'Is that because you're not sure our relationship will last?' I asked when he said no.

He looked horrified. 'No! It's because the costs are astronomical, and I can't ask you to spend a fortune on what is, effectively, a money pit. No matter how much is spent on it, it'll always need more.'

'But so does every home,' I said. 'All roofs leak at some stage. Walls crumble, paintwork chips, windows rattle, damp finds its way in, boilers need replacing.'

'Turrets tumble?' he quipped.

'Chimneys do,' I countered. 'What I'm saying is that Locke Keep is just like any other home in that they all need maintaining. Some more than others. And this is now my home, Ward, so if I can help ensure it doesn't fall down around our ears, and more importantly, that it'll still be standing when Eve marries and has children of her own, then surely that's a good thing? And you didn't ask. I offered.'

'Let me think about it,' he said.

I knew that he was battling with himself and his sense of pride and I understood that. But I continued to chip away at him, mainly by pointing out that some work was fairly urgent and that by spending money sooner rather than later it would save a fortune in the future, and he eventually agreed.

Work will be starting early next year, which means there'll be another 'building site' on Locke Isle, and not everyone on the island was pleased to hear that news.

They all want Locke Keep restored, but some people seem to think that magical creatures could transform the place overnight, and that towering scaffolds, teams of specialists, and many months of work, aren't necessary.

I head towards The Clothing Locker, where my friend Natalie works. That's another thing that's new for me. Having friends. Admittedly, I don't yet have one near my own age, apart from Ward, but at least I have friends. There's Tracy, and Natalie, and maybe now, Aggie.

I met Natalie on my first day on the island and although we're as different as chalk and cheese, and she's ten years younger than me, we get on really well. She's very pretty but doesn't know it, and to be honest, if she didn't scrape her jet black hair into such a tight bun, and didn't wear the long, false eyelashes that look as if a spider is crawling over her face, or paint her lips bright red making her pale complexion look somewhat sickly, she'd be beautiful. But I don't know her well enough to tell her those things yet. Which is another first for me. The old me wouldn't hesitate to tell someone what she thought of their appearance.

Natalie lives in Croft Cottage, which is near Castle Keep Hotel, with her daughter, Tilly, who is four, and her mum, Sharon, who is in her sixties and so bubbly that it's surprising the woman doesn't float away. Tilly's dad lived in Folkestone but as soon as Natalie told him she was pregnant, he ran off and joined the navy and he hasn't been seen since.

I offered to trace him for her, once she'd told me all about it, but she rejected the offer.

'We were only dating for about six months,' she said. 'If he loved me, or wanted to be a father, he wouldn't have run off.'

'But he should pay to help support Tilly,' I argued.

Natalie shook her head. 'I don't want his money. If he's not willing to offer it, I'm not going to force him to pay it.'

'Wouldn't it come in handy?' I asked, knowing full well that it would. Tracy and Roger told me that Natalie and her mum are struggling financially. But then so is everyone on the island. Or most of them, at least.

'It would. But we're managing.'

Tilly is a beautiful little girl with the same jet black hair as her mum, but she must have her dad's eyes because they're a startling hazel colour with flecks of pure gold. Or they seem to be. She could easily be a model for the children's clothing industry. I happen to know a few people in the business and I recently suggested to Natalie that I was certain I could get her a contract, thinking she would jump at the prospect of fame and fortune, if not for her then for Tilly. Instead she looked horrified.

'Thank you for the kind offer,' she said, 'but I want Tilly to have a normal life. Fame and all the stuff that goes with it isn't for us.'

Having a mum who is a supermodel, I

completely got what Natalie meant, so I let the subject drop.

I've tried to give Natalie money, but she won't take it and always looks hurt and embarrassed when I offer. I buy little gifts for Tilly, mainly small items of clothing and little toys, and I treat Natalie and Sharon to a spa day once a month at Castle Keep Hotel. I wanted it to be once a week but Natalie balked at that. Now I sometimes beg her to come with me more often, saying I don't want to go alone, and although I'm sure she knows exactly what I'm doing, she does agree from time to time.

The reindeers and all the other things on my Christmas list weren't just for Eve; they were also for Tilly. And, of course, all the other islanders. But Aggie is right about that. A day – or two – in Folkestone with everything it has to offer is probably as good. It'll definitely be considerably cheaper.

And yet I still can't help thinking how wonderful it would be to be able to nip down the road and see reindeer and penguins and Father Christmas, rather than having to take the ferry or water taxi over to Folkestone. Especially if the weather is bad. We've already had one freak storm and more are forecast for the last few weeks of December. Getting to Folkestone might not be as easy as it sounds.

'Hi, Nat,' I say as I open the door of The Clothing Locker, but it isn't Natalie who pops her head out from behind a red velvet curtain; it's Nell, the wife of Jonas Barnaby, the lighthouse keeper.

'Hello, Gen,' Nell trills. She sounds more like a bird than a human being ... and with her little beak nose and bright, beady eyes, she resembles one in a certain light. 'Nat's got the day off. Didn't she tell you? Although, now I think of it, she did say it was a snap decision. She's taken Tilly into Folkestone. Won't be back until the last water taxi run. And then, just between you and me, I think she's got a date. She didn't tell me that. I'm just putting two and two together and making a couple. Or should that be putting one and one together? Oh never mind. You know what I mean. Isn't it a lovely day? After that freak storm I thought we were in for a right old battering. My Jonas says we still may be. And you know what he's like with his weather. How are you today?'

I wait for a second or two to be sure that she's actually stopped talking and not just taking a breath.

'I'm fine, thanks. What makes you think Nat's got a date? She didn't mention one to me.'

'But she didn't mention she was taking today off, either, did she? And she is.'

'Yes. I see. I'll have to ask her when I see her. Erm. How are you? I hope the noise and dust and general mess from all the building work isn't causing you and Jonas too much discomfort.'

'Can't complain. It's got to be done. My Jonas says it'll all be worth it in the end. Just hard to tell when that might be. Don't suppose you've got any ides on that, have you? This cold weather makes my knees crack, especially if I go up and down a ladder. Or the stairs. And I don't like the dark mornings and dark nights. But there's nothing I can do about those. I can't wait for the shortest day to come and go so the nights start getting lighter. I'm more of a summer girl, you see. Now my Jonas, bless him, he loves all four seasons and doesn't give one more importance than another. How's Ward? Such a handsome man, isn't he? You make the perfect couple, what with you being such a beauty. My Jonas says you could sink ships with those looks.' She giggles like a girl of eight. 'Let's hope it's not the ferry. Or the water taxi. Now that Grady's a handsome one too, isn't he? Did I hear someone say you once dated his older brother? Does he look like Grady? Reminds me of Tom Cruise. Oh, I love Tom Cruise, don't you? My Jonas was the spitting image of him when he was younger. You've probably noticed the resemblance.'

Jonas Barnaby is a lovely man, and I'm sure some people would call him handsome. But he is no Tom Cruise, believe me, and the only resemblance that I can possibly see is that Jonas has sported those Ray-Ban Aviator sunglasses from time to time during this summer.

'Uh-huh,' I lie. 'As for Adam – Grady's brother – that was so long ago I can't really remember what he looks like. But you're right. Grady does remind me of Tom Cruise. I think it's his smile. And his eyes. And maybe, his hair. Erm.' I cough to clear my throat – and to stop remembering exactly what Adam looked like, because that man could've earnt a living as Tom Cruise's double ... only younger. 'I'm sorry about your knees. As for the building work, the worst of it should be almost done before they shut down for Christmas but it depends on the weather. It was lovely chatting, Nell, but I've just remembered that Ward and Aggie are expecting me. We're going to be discussing our plans for Christmas.' In about four hours' time, but I need an excuse to get out of here.

'You're making plans for Christmas? What fun! Christmas is always a fairly quiet affair. There's the carol concert at the church and carol singing around the island, but that's about it. My Jonas wouldn't bother with fairy lights, but he knows I love them so he makes the effort. And Main Road always looks festive with a string of lights and a small tree. Oh, I do hope you're planning something special.'

Now here's a woman who would appreciate the reindeer, penguins, and Elves.

But I think, like me, she's going to be disappointed.

Five

I can't help wondering why Nell thinks Natalie has a date tonight and I'm tempted to text Nat and ask her. But Nell said Nat was taking Tilly to Folkestone for the day so I don't want to interrupt their fun day out.

As I head home, I consider nipping down to the beach to see what's going on. I could've sworn I heard a helicopter when I was in The Clothing Locker chatting to Nell and I wasn't aware of any deliveries arriving today. I like to keep on top of such things and have given strict instructions for the site manager to notify me of any updates to the schedule, but when I check my phone, there isn't a text or an email from him.

The problem is, it's freezing out here, and I think I need to pee. Cold weather doesn't usually have any effect on me – or my bladder – I go skiing every year and I've been to Antarctica, and the Arctic, for heaven's sake – but this island appears to have a climate all of its own.

The day I arrived, we got caught in a sudden storm halfway across the Channel. A squall, it's called. The wind was howling and the rain was torrential and the ferry rocked and groaned and if it hadn't been for Ward's calm and controlled manner I might've feared for my life. I think, for a second, I did. But he told me to look out of the wheelhouse window and I saw Locke Isle bathed in sunshine. Yet we were a mere five minutes away.

And today, it's the other way around. Dark clouds are hanging over the island, but Folkestone sits beneath a blue sky and sunshine. I bet it's still cold over there though, and not a day to sit outside on the Harbour Arm at The Lighthouse Champagne Bar quaffing bubbly. Although…

No. I mustn't be tempted by the delights of Folkestone.

Maybe tomorrow.

I hurry home and I'm shivering as I dash into the sitting room. Ward smiles at me in a way that tells me he's both pleased and relieved to see me. I've only been gone for about an hour, so my heart fills with joy at his reaction to my return.

'Gen!' he yells. 'You're home!' I'm only a few feet away from him now, so I'm not sure why his voice is raised. And then I see the reason for his odd behaviour and I can't believe my eyes.

'Dad!' Now I'm the one shrieking. 'What on earth are you doing here? And why didn't you tell me you were coming?'

Dad smiles triumphantly, as if he wanted to throw me off balance and he's achieved his goal. Which he certainly has.

'Hello Geneva,' he says his voice dripping honey. I know that voice. It's one he uses when he wants to get his own way. And that is most of the time. 'It's good to see you too.'

'Erm. Yes. This is a lovely surprise. Erm. I see you've met Ward.' I hold my hand out and Ward takes it. That gives me some comfort and also some much-needed support.

'I have,' Dad says smoothly, and then leans down and gently brushes something from his suit jacket and trousers. He's wearing one of his most expensive suits from Saville Row so he clearly intended to impress anyone crossing his path today. 'And I've just met Eve and ... Horatio.'

He gives Ward a tight smile that tells me he would rather like to strangle both Eve and Horatio, and a snort of laughter mixed with a gasp of horror escapes me. I cover it with a cough, just as Eve and Horatio race from her room. She's brandishing a plastic cutlass and

Horatio is dribbling as he sometimes does when he's overexcited.

'Is this your dad?' Eve asks, poking Dad with the tip of her cutlass.

'Eve!' Ward snaps. 'Didn't I just tell you that it's rude to do that?'

Eve nods and grins up at Dad, who, to my utter astonishment, grins back.

'Sorry,' Eve says.

'I'll live,' says Dad.

'Yes,' I say. 'At least I think it is. Erm. Have you been here long, Dad?' I ask darting a look at Ward who shakes his head.

'No,' Dad says. 'Although it does feel as if I have. I arrived a few minutes before you. I'd have waited outside if I'd known you would soon appear.'

'If you'd let me know you were coming, you wouldn't have needed to wait. Please sit down, Dad. Would you like tea or coffee?

'Do you have anything stronger?' he asks, eyeing the comfy but worn sofa and the cushions scattered all over it as if something life threatening might be lurking there.

'Whisky?' Ward offers.

'Perfect. Thank you,' says Dad. He looks at his suit once more and then, with an almost inaudible sigh, but one I can hear, he perches on the edge of the seat.

'Wine?' Ward asks me as he turns towards the kitchen.

'Large,' I say and then, before I have time to stop her, Eve leaps onto the sofa and sits right beside Dad and Horatio jumps up and sits beside her. Both of them stare at Dad who looks more uncomfortable than I've ever seen him look in his life.

'Well isn't this … cosy?' Dad says, looking at me as if I'm on his death-list too.

'It is good to see you,' I say, trying hard not to laugh as he attempts to lean away from Eve and she moves closer still.

I was surprised when, back in September, once I plucked up the courage to tell Dad that I was staying on Locke Isle and resigning from the company, Dad said he must come and see the place for himself. After he blew his top, that is. But I didn't really expect him to come. And definitely not so soon.

'I was in the neighbourhood,' he says. 'I thought it was the perfect opportunity to see the place you think is so wonderful that you're prepared to leave your own apartment, your beloved Edinburgh, and the company, not to mention your family, to dash off and live there.'

I think it was the mention of "family" that surprised me. We're more like business colleagues who just happen to be related.

'Did you come by helicopter?' I ask.

'Yes,' he replies. 'Is there another mode

of transport?'

'The ferry,' Eve says, tapping his knee with her cutlass. 'And also the water taxi. That's not a car, it's a boat. And the ferry is really a pirate ship.'

Dad raises one brow ever so slightly. 'I see,' he says. 'If only I'd known.'

Ward returns with a tray of drinks. Wine for me, whisky for him and Dad, an orange juice for Eve, and a bowl of water for Horatio which he places on the floor near the sofa.

Dad looks at him in astonishment.

'Cheers,' says Ward, sitting down beside me on a sofa opposite Dad, Eve and Horatio and holding up his whisky tumbler. At least he's used the best crystal glasses. 'It really is a pleasure to meet you.'

'Oh. Yes, cheers,' says Dad taking a large gulp of his drink.

'Cheers,' Eve repeats.

'Cheers!' I take several gulps of mine. I still can't believe Dad's here. 'So … where did the helicopter land?' I venture.

'On what I assume you intend to be the helipad,' Dad replies.

'Helipad?' queries Ward, shooting a look at me.

'The roof of the boat house,' I say, shaking my head.

'Boat house?' Dad grins. 'How interesting. But then this is such an interesting place, isn't it, Geneva? I discovered, just the other day, that your former Nanny has a cottage – and a husband – here. It's such a small world. I assume you've been in touch?'

I can feel Ward staring at me no doubt wondering why I hadn't had the courage to tell Dad about Tracy and Roger.

'Yes. Didn't I mention that I was coming to stay with them?'

Our eyes meet and lock and there's a twitch at the side of Dad's mouth, because we both know full well that I didn't.

'I may have missed that,' he says equably.

'I might have forgotten to mention it. Sorry.'

'Ah well. I know now. And I can see why you find Locke Isle so ... enticing. From what I've seen of it so far, it's a very special place. Who knew such a treasure was sitting here in the middle of the English Channel?'

'It's been in my family for centuries,' Ward says, sitting upright in a rather defensive manner.

'Has it?' Dad is wearing one of his, 'I want this place' expressions.

'Yes,' I say. 'And it's not for sale and never will be. Plus, I understand there are restrictive covenants forbidding ownership of property on the island by anyone other than a resident of Locke Isle. So it wouldn't be much use to anyone other than someone who wants to live here.'

Dad nods and smiles. 'I see. It's probably a lovely place to live. Is it, Geneva? You've been here for, oh, what is it? Three months now?'

'Getting on for four. And yes. It's a magical place to live. I love it here.'

'Even with all that building work going on? I hear there's going to be a new promenade and jetty. And a harbour arm? Plus, of course, the boat house you mentioned. You're shoring up the cliffs I see, in an effort to halt the coastal erosion. That can't be cheap.'

'I … we … got a good bargain.'

'Yes. Francis always did have a soft spot for you, didn't he? Do give him my regards next time you see him.'

'I shall. Are you … are you planning on staying the night, Dad?'

'No,' he says, a little too quickly. 'Sorry, Geneva. Business calls. Especially since I'm short-staffed these days. You know how it is.'

'I do. It's a shame you must rush off. I could've shown you around. And I'm sure you would have loved to have said hello to Tracy after all these years.'

His eyes narrow just a fraction. 'Yes. That is a pity. But … I don't have to rush off right now. I have an hour or so to spare. And it would be such a pleasure to see more of Locke Isle. I can rest easy at night knowing my only daughter has found her own little slice of paradise. And has fallen in love. Yet again.'

'No, Dad. Not again. I've fallen in love for the first time. Truly in love. Deeply in love. And forever.'

'Erm. Is something going on here that I should know about?' Ward asks, clasping my hand tightly and glancing from me to Dad and back again while Eve stares up at Dad, with a questioning frown.

Dad meets my eye and then slowly smiles and empties his glass. 'I believe you have, Geneva. And although it's a surprise. I couldn't be happier for you both.

Eve pokes Dad's leg with the cutlass. 'Are you going to be my grandad?'

Ward, Dad and I all look at one another in turn.

'I think that rather depends on my daughter, little one. And on your dad, of course. But if things turn out the way I believe they both hope they will, I suppose the answer is yes.'

'Are you coming back for Christmas then?'

'Sadly not. I'll be in Aspen for Christmas. I assume you know where Aspen is?'

Eve frowns but nods. 'It's in America.'

Dad looks pleased. 'It is. And you're all welcome to visit whenever you like.'

'Really?' Eve bounces up and down on the sofa. 'Horatio too?'

Dad throws a look at the dog. 'Horatio too. You can use the company jet.'

'You've got a jet? And a helicopter? Do you have a ship as well?'

'I have a yacht,' says Dad. 'but I rarely use that these days.'

'Wow!' says Eve, clearly impressed. 'And I thought Gen was rich! Do you have more money than the King?'

'Eve!' Ward says. 'That's enough.'

Dad smiles, leans towards her, and nods.

I don't know who this man is, but he can't possibly be my dad.

And then his phone rings and he answers it immediately, curses loudly, apologises to Ward for that and jumps to his feet, putting his empty glass on the table.

'I'm so sorry but I'm afraid I do have to leave right now, after all. Perhaps I could come again?'

Ward glances briefly at me and then says, 'You're welcome at any time.'

'It would be lovely to see you again, Dad. But maybe you could call and let us know next time?'

'I'll do that. Will you walk me out,

Geneva?'

'Of course.'

'Goodbye, little one,' Dad says to Eve. He even nods at Horatio.

This has been the weirdest experience, ever.

I grab my coat and lead the way down to the front doors. 'I'll walk with you to the helicopter,' I say.

'That would be nice,' he replies, and we walk down the stone steps in silence.

'Did you know Ward before you came here?' Dad suddenly asks.

'No. I met him for the first time when he brought me over on the ferry. He owns that, and at the time, was the ferry captain. But now he's found someone to take over. Oh. You know him. It's Grady.'

'Grady Walsh? Adam's younger brother?'

'Yep. You're right about it being a small world, Dad.'

'Does Ward know about Adam?'

'Yep. But there's nothing to tell. That was over years ago.'

'I liked Adam. But you're weren't suited.' He stops and looks at me. 'Ward is more your type. Try not to mess this one up, Geneva. If you genuinely believe Ward is the one, do whatever you need to do to make it work.'

'I will, Dad. Why did you ask if I knew

him before?'

'Because you look as if you've known one another for a long time. Now I'd better fly. Literally. That deal you were working on before you left looks as if it might fall at the last hurdle, and I can't have that.'

'Dad. I'm sorry if I left you in the lurch. Do you … do you need me to help out for a while? I can. If you do.'

'No. Go and follow your dreams, Geneva. I know I rarely show it, but I do love you, you know. I want you to be happy.'

I definitely can't believe this man is my dad, and when he climbs a ladder to get to the roof of the skeleton of what will be the boat house, and then blows me a kiss as the helicopter takes off, I'm even more astonished.

Perhaps us being apart for a few months and me leaving the company is something I should've done years ago. Or maybe Dad is simply being swept up by the festive spirit. Although he never seemed to like Christmas much before.

Six

'That was a surprise,' Ward says later as he and I walk hand-in-hand to Aggie's cottage for afternoon tea, having dropped Eve and Horatio at Tracy and Roger's. 'And I don't just mean your dad turning up unannounced. I mean the fact that he wasn't at all how I'd imagined he would be.'

'You're not the only one who is surprised, believe me. The man you met today was definitely not the dad I've known all my life. In fact, he was the complete opposite.'

Ward smiles at me and squeezes my hand. 'You came here because you wanted to change. Perhaps your dad wants to change too.'

'It's possible, I suppose. Anything is possible. But we'll have to see what he's like the next time he visits. Assuming there is a next time. And with Dad, I wouldn't bet on it.'

Ward pulls up his collar and then mine with his free hand. 'It's getting colder. And the wind is picking up. I wouldn't be surprised if we have another storm before morning.'

'I hope it snows,' I say. 'I bet Locke Isle looks magical covered in fluffy white snow.'

'It may look magical but we'd have to use the ferry to do the crossings. Using the water taxi wouldn't be safe if it snows. I was caught in a heavy snowfall once when the snow came down fast and I couldn't see a thing. Luckily for me I was almost home but it wasn't a pleasant experience, and that was in the ferry. The English Channel is the world's busiest shipping lane and Locke Isle is smack bang in the middle of the narrowest stretch, so extra care needs to be taken in any type of bad weather.'

'Oh. I'd assumed it was just heavy rain storms, or gales that would put the water taxi out of action. I hadn't considered snow. Would that mean, that if we had a lot of snow, not even the ferry would run?'

Ward nods. 'That's right. We could cross in between snowfalls but as you experienced on your first trip, storms can blow in from nowhere and take us by surprise. That includes snow storms. Safety must always come first.'

'So ... we could be snowed-in on the

island for days? Or weeks? Or even months?'

'We could. But it's unlikely here in the UK. The longest I can ever remember the ferry being grounded, so to speak, was for about four days. We all stock up for the winter so if one of us runs out of something, someone else is likely to have that thing to spare.'

'I remember laughing when you told me that in September. I said we'd be like the bears and hibernate for the winter. I hadn't taken it seriously though.'

'I know.' He laughs. 'So it's a good thing you're living with me, isn't it? Because I've been a good little bear, as always, and stocked up on everything we might need.'

'Including my moisturiser? And shampoo? And … tampons?'

'Yep. Even those. Although not your exact moisturiser, so if you want a particular brand, you'd better order some in while you can. And that's another reason I don't think bringing living creatures – or even extra people – over to the island in December is a good idea. What if we have a storm and they all get stuck here for days or weeks? Finding food for them all might cause a major problem if we can't make the trip to the mainland.'

'You know what? That airline doesn't sound like such a bad idea after all.'

'Even planes are grounded in bad weather, Gen. You know that. Welcome to life on an island.'

'Thanks. I should've read the small print.'

He stops suddenly and spins me round to face him. 'It's unlikely to be a problem, Gen. Really. There's nothing to worry about. You're not … you're not having second thoughts are you?'

'What?' I laugh in astonishment. 'Of course not. Oh, Ward. It'll take a lot more than bad weather to make me regret moving here. In fact, I don't think there's anything that could ever make me regret that. I love you, Ward. Even my dad could see that.'

'I love you too,' he says. 'Erm. What did you think when Eve asked if he was going to be her grandad?' He slips his free arm around my waist and then lets go of my hand and slips the other arm around me. He holds me tightly and pulls me close.

'I almost choked, but I thought it was sweet. I was amazed by Dad's response though.'

Ward smiles and tips his head to one side. 'You realise that for him to become her official grandad, you and I should be married, don't you?'

I'm speechless for a second. Is he … is he asking me to marry him?

His muscles tense and his jaw tightens. 'You're right,' he continues. 'It's far too soon to be thinking about that. We'd better get a move on or Aggie will wonder where we are.' He turns and steps forward and he doesn't take my hand this time.

'Ward?'

'Yes?'

He doesn't stop walking so I hurry after him.

'I didn't say it was too soon. I didn't say anything at all.'

'I know,' he says, without looking at me. 'That's the problem.'

Before I can say another word, Jonas Barnaby rides into view on his bicycle.

'Afternoon,' he says. 'There's a storm coming.'

'Tell me about it,' I say under my breath.

Ward says, 'I thought there might be. I'd better call Grady and let him know.'

'He's an experienced sailor, Ward,' I say. 'He's sailed the seven seas. And everything in between.'

'But unless he's sailed a ferry or water taxi across this stretch of water several times in all weathers, he may not be prepared for what could hit him. As I said earlier, safety comes first. I realise you think he and his brother are invincible, but he might get a nasty shock.'

'What? I've never said that,' I protest, but Ward is looking at Jonas.

'You're right about that,' says Jonas, and then he looks at me. 'Many a sailor's come a cropper between this island and the mainland. It's not just Elizabeth Locke and Grifforde Betancourt who've drowned in these waters.'

'Who?'

'It's an old tale about my ancestors,' Ward says. 'It's not important right now. Thanks, Jonas. Take care.'

'Well that's a cheery thought,' I say.

'Look,' says Ward, stopping just before we reach Aggie's door. 'Do you think you and Aggie could do this without me? Aggie knows what I'd be happy with. If there's another storm on the way there're a few things I need to do.'

'Erm. Of course. Anything I can do to help?'

'No. Apart from promise me you'll remove all living things from that list of yours. I've got enough to worry about without reindeer and penguins and Elves being trapped here, or drowning on the journey.'

He doesn't wait for me to answer and he doesn't smile or kiss me when he walks away.

'And a very Merry Christmas to you too!' I shout after him.

But the wind is really picking up now and he either doesn't hear me, or he's choosing to ignore me.

Seven

'We need to talk,' I say when I eventually make it back to Locke Keep around 6 p.m. and stumble into the sitting room. Ward is clearly astonished to see me.

I'm dripping wet, my hair's a complete mess, with twigs and leaves and god knows what else in it, and I'm covered in mud where I slipped and fell more than once on my journey home.

I now know what it might feel like to be one of those little metal balls on a pinball machine. For the last thirty minutes or so the wind has been shoving me from pillar to post – and it should only have been a ten-minute walk at most from Aggie's cottage.

'What are you doing here?' Ward is seriously cross. 'I told you to stay at Aggie's and I'd come and get you when the storm dies down.'

His phone rings and he glares at me and then at the screen.

'It's probably Aggie,' I say. 'I left her a note.'

'You left…? What?' He answers the call. 'Yes. I know. I'm cross too. She's here and she's safe.' His eyes scan me from head to toe. 'I think. Sorry to worry you. Yes. She is a fool. I've got to go. We'll talk later.' He rings off, folds his arms across his chest and stares at me. 'Well?'

'I'm a fool!' I repeat.

'Yes.'

'That wasn't a question. That was a contradiction. I'm not a fool. You are.'

'How very mature. Why did you leave Aggie's?'

'Because … because you told me not to come home.'

He scowls at me. 'That makes total sense. Why would you ever do what I tell you? Even when I have your best interest and your safety at heart.'

'How was I to know the storm was as bad as it is?'

'Perhaps because I told you it was?'

'Why are you shouting?' Eve asks, popping her head around the door and looking concerned.

'We're not,' says Ward lowering his voice. 'Sorry, honey. We've just raised our voices because we're trying to get one another to see the other's point of view. But that never works, so we'll stop. Go and finish your supper and I'll be with you in a moment.'

'Why are you all wet and muddy?' Eve asks me. 'Were you caught in the storm?'

'Yes,' I say, lowering my voice too. 'And it was my fault. I should've listened to your dad.'

'Oh sh … I mean, sugar. You *are* soaking wet and you're shivering. Go and get undressed and I'll run you a warm bath and make you a hot drink. And yes. I am telling you what to do again but this time I hope you'll listen.'

I nod because I can see he's genuinely concerned and also because he's no longer angry, just anxious.

'Thank you,' I say. 'But is there any chance of a hot bath and a glass of mulled wine? I had some at Aggie's and it was delicious.'

He smiles at me and guides me gently towards the main bathroom where the bath is large enough for both of us … and maybe even a humpback whale.

'Your wish is my command,' he says.

'If only that were true. Sorry. I'm going.'

He follows me in, turns on the taps and adds just the right amount of my favourite, Neom Magnesium Bath Milk while I slowly peel off my sodden clothes.

At another time and in different circumstances this would be incredibly sexy, but I'm freezing cold and Eve is just a few doors away in the kitchen.

Nevertheless, once I'm naked, he glances at me and sucks in a long breath and then he coughs and looks away, picking up my discarded clothes from the floor.

'I'll be back in a second,' he says without looking back.

I slide beneath the water and it immediately works its magic. I close my eyes and let my mind drift off to an evening when Ward and I did share this bath, and I now wish Eve was fast asleep and not still eating her supper.

I shouldn't have been cross with Ward. When he called me and told me to stay at Aggie's, part of me thought he'd done that because of the way we'd parted earlier. So naturally, I'd done the opposite and made my way home. Aggie had gone to take a phone call and I'd scribbled her a brief note and dashed out.

But Ward had told me to stay because, unlike me, he'd realised how dangerous it might be to venture out in this storm.

The walls of this place are at least fifteen inches thick and yet I can hear the wind howling and branches snapping and the torrential rain lashing the windows. It's actually getting worse.

At least I'm glad I left when I did, but I'll have to call Aggie and apologise. I'll have to apologise to Ward as well.

When will I learn that Ward often knows better?

'Here you are,' he says, carrying a heat-proof glass filled almost to the brim with mulled wine. 'Feeling better?'

'Much.' I take the glass by the handle and sip the contents. 'Heaven,' I say and I smile up at him.

'You know how much I want to get in there with you, don't you?' he says.

'I know how much I'd like you to,' I reply. 'But, as a matter of interest, would a humpback whale fit in this bath?'

He snorts a laugh and shakes his head. 'I love you, Gen, but you drive me nuts sometimes.'

'Ditto,' I say. 'And don't worry. All living creatures have been removed from my Christmas list.'

He eyes me suspiciously. 'What about the pool, the Elves, and Santa's village?'

'All gone.'

'The ski slope and the ice rink?'

'The ice rink will only be a small one and it's like the ones you see in shopping centres and town squares. It sort of pops up, I believe, with hardly any effort involved at all.'

'Fine. And the trees?'

I smile. 'Smaller. And fewer. But I can't cross everything off the list, Ward. It is my first Christmas here after all and I do want it to be a little special. But Aggie has told me that less is often more and I've taken that on board. There are now only about ten, maybe twelve. Fourteen at most, items remaining. And we can talk about those in bed tonight.'

'Oh can we?' he says, with that sexy grin of his spreading across his face as he leans forward and kisses me. 'I had something else in mind.'

Eight

'Why are the church bells so loud this morning?' I turn over and pull a pillow over my head. I didn't get much sleep last night, partly due to the storm and partly thanks to Ward, but I didn't mind him keeping me awake one bit. 'I know it's the second Sunday in Advent, but really? Are they always this loud?'

'Those aren't the church bells.' Ward tosses back the covers and leaps out of bed. 'That's the siren on the fire engine.' I sit up and lean back against the headboard while he checks his phone and he curses under his breath. Then he runs a hand through his hair and sighs loudly. 'I'm always lecturing you about listening to me, but I should've listened to you.' He swivels round and looks me in the eye. 'It's gone, Gen. The seaward section of the Boardwalk has broken in half and some of it's been swept out into the Channel and some of it's been dumped on the beach by the waves.'

'Oh no! What does that mean? That the ferry can't dock there?'

He nods and sighs again, shaking his head this time. 'It's been there for years. It's had storms and gales and even boats crashing into it and yet it's held its own. Until last night.'

'What about the water taxi? Can that moor beside the part that's left?'

'I don't know. I'll have to go and see. But from the photos Jonas has sent me, I doubt it. Will you look after Eve until I get back? I don't know how long I'll be.'

'Of course. Unless you want me to come with you. The guys and girls on site might be able to offer some help.'

'It's Sunday, Gen. There won't be anyone on site today. And if we can't sort something out with the Boardwalk and the jetty, there may not be anyone on site for the foreseeable future.'

'But ... we need to get the work finished before Christmas.'

'Then you'd better add one large miracle to that Christmas list of yours, because that's what we'll need.'

He stands up, turns around and comes and kisses me and then he hurries to the shower.

I phone Tracy to ask her if she can see

the damage to the Boardwalk from her window and when she doesn't answer, I worry that some of the cliff might have collapsed last night too but as panic is setting in, she calls me back.

'Sorry, sweetheart,' she says. 'I was outside with Roger surveying the damage. Have you heard? I assume Ward has? The Boardwalk has gone. Been swept away like a matchstick. And so has the Watershed. Smashed to smithereens and most of it's flown off somewhere. It's probably landed in one of the other gardens. I hope it hasn't caused any damage.'

'Oh I'm so sorry about that,' I say.

The Watershed is – or should I say, was – Roger's fold-up wooden bar in their garden. I can imagine how upset he must be because he loved that little sanctuary of his, as did Tracy.

I'll add a new one of those to my list of presents.

If only adding a jetty was that simple.

'But here I am worrying about Roger's bar,' Tracy's continues. 'What I should be worrying about is the ferry and the water taxi. I know Ward and Grady got them moored safely in Folkestone before the storm took hold, and then Grady brought Ward back here on the water taxi and then returned to Folkestone. Ward told me that when he collected Eve. But are they okay, do you know? From the local news it seems the storm was mainly centred in the Channel. The mainland appears to have got off Scot-free, but I wondered if the swell hit the coast.'

'I don't know. Ward hasn't mentioned them this morning. I hope Grady made it safely back.'

'He did. He phoned Ward as soon as he'd tied up to the moorings, so I know he was safe. It only takes a few minutes to do the crossing in that motor launch. That really was a wonderful gift to us all, sweetheart.'

'It was a gift to me too. It means I don't have to travel on the smelly, rolling ferry. Diesel fumes aren't my favourite. The water taxi is luxury compared to that. Was there any damage to your cottage? Or to any others that you can see?'

'Thankfully, I don't think so. There may be a few tiles loose here and there and some fences down, and sheds, like ours, smashed to pieces, but the cottages have stood for at least a hundred years, some even longer. This isn't the first storm that's swept through here, and it won't be the last. I thought some of the cliff might have gone but it seems the work on the site that's been done already might've helped shore it up. There'll be a few people thanking you today, Geneva.'

'I don't want thanks. I just wish I

could've – we could've – saved the jetty.'

'Yes. Roger says it might be a problem.'

'I think that's an understatement. But there must be something we can do. Wait! Dad visited yesterday and he used the roof of the boat house to land. Well, his pilot did. That means we can, at least, get some of the workforce out here the same way. By helicopter.'

'You can't just go out and buy a helicopter, can you? Or do you rent them? Wait a moment! Did you just say your dad visited yesterday? Ward didn't mention that. Did he meet him?'

'Yes. And you won't believe it but Dad was a completely changed man. Or perhaps it was only for yesterday. We'll have to see. Ward probably had the storm on his mind when he collected Eve. Or maybe he felt it was up to me to tell you. Anyway, as for the helicopter, they can be purchased or rented. But I happen to know a man who owns one.'

'Your dad?'

'My dad. This will tell if he's really changed his spots. Ward's coming out of the shower so I'd better go. Can I pop in and see you later?'

'Anytime, sweetheart. You know you're always welcome. Give Ward our love.'

'Will do.' I ring off. 'Ward! I think I may have an answer to our predicament.'

'Oh? I'm all ears. Who was that on the phone?'

'Tracy. I called to see how they are. But that can wait. Dad owns a helicopter, Ward.'

He furrows his brows. 'Is this really the time?'

I sigh. 'A helicopter. Remember? He landed it here yesterday.'

'I'm not senile ... oh, I see. Are you saying he might help us get labour and materials here? Would he do that?'

'I can ask.'

'But hasn't he gone back to Edinburgh?'

'Nope. Not yet. The deal he was here for is just along the coast, and it's close to one of Dad's favourite hotels. One of his own, that is. So he'll have spent the night. I'll call him around 9.30 and see what he says.'

'Why 9.30? Is he a late riser?'

I laugh at that. 'He'll have been up since 5 a.m. but he has a routine and woe betide anyone who interrupts that.'

Nine

'I'll be happy to help you, Geneva,' Dad says. 'But when I say that, you do of course understand that I mean, by the loan of my helicopter and my pilot. Not by me actually doing anything myself.'

'I'm your daughter, Dad. I know exactly what you mean. And thank you. This means a great deal to us.'

'Think nothing of it. How long will you be needing it?'

'I'm not sure. Until we can think of a way to make some sort of structure so that the ferry, or at the very least the water taxi, can dock and let passengers on and off.'

'I'm surprised at you, Geneva? Surely you've considered pontoons?'

'Pontoons? Of course. Pontoons! Why didn't I think of that?'

'That's precisely what I'm asking. Why didn't you? Never mind. You'll still be needing the helicopter to transport them from A to B. Unless you take them across on the ferry, or the company delivers them. But you'll need people to assemble them to make a jetty. The helicopter is yours for a week. After that I'll be needing it back in Edinburgh. Although I can probably make do without it. Let me know how things go.'

'Thanks, Dad. Oh. Any news on that deal?'

'Back on track. I'll tell Jonno you'll be needing him and the helicopter. Do you need him today? Or is tomorrow soon enough? I believe, as I planned to remain here today, he was taking the day off. But one call can change that.'

'No! Tomorrow is fine. I'll make some calls and get everyone organised this end and then I'll text him the details first thing in the morning. Thanks again, Dad.'

'You're welcome, Geneva. Good luck with it all.'

'Well,' I say to Ward when I ring off. 'I don't know what in the world has happened to my dad but I truly hope he stays this way. We can have the helicopter for a week but he reminded me about pontoons and they will solve the problem on a temporary basis.'

'I heard you say that. Like the ones in Folkestone? They had them at the old harbour, I believe, to form a bridge for vehicles to get on and off the ships going to and from the western front. They may still be there. But where do we get pontoons now?'

'No idea. But the internet will know. Or Francis and his team will. I'm sure we can hire them. I think Dad used them once when he was having a resort built in a lagoon.'

'As you do,' says Ward, raising his eyebrows. 'You and your dad live in a completely different world from the rest of us, don't you?'

Now I raise my brows. 'Says the man who lives in a thousand-or-so-year-old fortress and owns an island in the middle of the English Channel.'

'Yes. But I'm cash-poor.'

'And you're always telling Eve that money isn't everything.'

'It is when you need a pontoon or four. I don't suppose the things will be cheap. Or buy one, get one free.'

'Unlikely. But what's the point of having money if you can't spend it on the things you want?'

'I've always wanted a pontoon for Christmas,' Ward quips. 'Far more useful than socks.'

Ten

In case you ever need them, pontoons can be hired from right here in the UK. The company even has out-of-hours contacts, so we call one of the numbers listed, right away. Not only is the chap we speak to, super-knowledgeable, he's also super-helpful. He tells us precisely how many pontoons we need and how long it'll take for his specialist team to construct our jetty. As luck would have it, he is both willing and able to fit this job in as a rush order.

The men arrive first thing on Monday morning. It is pouring with rain when they step onto the beach but as is often the case here, the weather changes and the sun comes out half an hour later.

The sea is calm today and as Ward and I, along with all the other islanders have cleared all the storm debris from the beach, it doesn't look as if gale force winds battered the island on Saturday night. Apart from the fact that the Boardwalk is no longer an L-shape jutting out into the sea.

Grady brings the water taxi across and manages to moor at the side of what is left of the jetty, which is basically a small stub standing on just two remaining posts. It's far from ideal and the sooner the pontoon jetty is built the better.

Thanks to Jonno and Dad's helicopter, along with Grady and the water taxi, the workforce for the new Boardwalk is brought over to the island and cracks on. They have been staying on the island during the week but returning to their homes on Saturday afternoons and coming back to the island on Mondays. They had all left for the weekend prior to the arrival of the storm, but they are welcomed back with renewed enthusiasm by all the residents of Locke Isle and anyone would have thought they had been gone for weeks.

I take Eve to school in Folkestone via helicopter. She is thrilled and excited and has now decided that she might like to be a helicopter pilot in addition to a pirate captain.

I think I'll collect her via water taxi. Ward has agreed to the small pirate ship as a gift for her for Christmas but he will draw the line at a helicopter. And so might I.

Although Ward and I have agreed on two

things thanks to everything that happened over the weekend. The boat house isn't too big. And the roof should be a helipad. Just in case of emergencies. Or visits from my dad.

As Ward has everything under control and knows as much as I do about pontoons, I leave him to deal with the jetty and, after checking that Francis' team have all they need, I go and have coffee with Tracy.

After an hour or so chatting and inspecting the area of garden where the Watershed once stood, I go and see if Natalie is free for lunch.

'I want to hear all about your day in Folkestone,' I say when we're seated in Fifi's, the French restaurant on Main Road and we both have a glass of wine in front of us. Fifi's opens for lunch and dinner but it's always half empty at lunchtime.

I'm surprised when Natalie blushes.

'It was lovely,' she says.

'Was it just you and Tilly, or did your mum go too?'

'Mum didn't go.'

I fiddle with the stem of my glass, silently debating with myself whether I should mention my conversation with Nell.

'Nell said she thought you had a date in the evening.'

Nat's mouthful of wine shoots across the table and she nearly chokes.

'Oh, God! I'm so sorry Nat.'

She shakes her head. 'No, no. I'm the one who should be sorry for embarrassing you.'

'You haven't embarrassed me. I've done that hundreds of times. Don't worry about it.' I pour her more wine from the bottle I'd ordered. 'But did you?' I ask before she takes a gulp.

She looks me in the eye and blushes profusely.

'Don't be mad,' she eventually says.

'Why would I be mad? Unless you're going to tell me it was with Ward. Only as he was with me, I know it can't have been.'

She shakes her head. 'It was with Grady.'

'Grady? Grady Walsh?'

She nods and takes several gulps of wine. 'Only it wasn't much of a date because of the storm. Ward called him and said they needed to get the ferry and the water taxi safely moored in Folkestone. Tilly was at a friend's house for the afternoon, which is why I was with Grady, so I went to collect her right away and Grady brought us back.'

'Oh. Erm. Well that's all good. He's entitled to take time off. You're single. He's single. There's not much of an age difference. Not that it matters if there was. But ... why would you think I'd be mad?'

'Because he said you dated his older brother and he dumped you.'

'Did he? Well, that's true. Adam wanted to work somewhere warm. I wanted to stay in Edinburgh. Plus, we weren't really suited. Even my dad thought that. But I don't know why that would make me mad. I didn't love Adam and we didn't date for long. I wasn't particularly upset when he left.'

'Oh? Erm. Grady seems to think you were. In fact ... erm ... I'm not sure if I should say this. Please don't tell Grady I have. He said that he thinks one of the reasons you wanted him for this job is because you're hoping Adam might come to visit him and then ... you could ... catch up.'

'Oh did he, indeed!' Now I am cross. But Nat looks terrified and I realise that she's told me this in confidence. 'Don't worry. I won't say anything. But perhaps, if you're seeing Grady again, you might tell him that we had a chat about how much I adore Ward. Because I do. And how I know Ward is the only man I'll ever love, or want, or need.'

'Of course. I'll tell him that. Exactly that.'

'I like Grady, Nat. But I hadn't realised he thinks I'm holding a candle for his brother and that was one of the reasons he got the job. It was Ward's decision. Not mine. Will you also tell him that? I'd hate it if he tells anyone else what he's told you. Especially as it's not true.'

She nods frantically. 'Of course. Yes. I'll

make sure he knows.'

'Erm. It's none of my business but when did Grady ask you out?'

'The first day we met.' She blushes again. 'The day he started his job as captain. Tilly and I had been to the birthday party of the same friend she was with on Saturday, so we'd gone over on the water taxi. It was when we were coming home on the last trip of the evening that he asked me. I said no at first because … well, because he's absolutely gorgeous and I couldn't see what a man like him could see in me, especially as I have Tilly. But he asked me out every time we met after that, and on Friday I finally said yes to a date for Saturday afternoon. It was supposed to be for the evening too, but, well, the storm arrived.'

'Firstly, Nat. You're gorgeous too. And so is Tilly. Any man would be lucky to have you in his life. And secondly, are you glad you said yes?'

She shrugs. 'Yes. And no. I think I could easily fall in love with him, but he's been everywhere and done everything. I've lived my entire life on Locke Isle. And I work in a clothes shop. I'm not sure what we have in common.'

'Opposites attract, so they say. I'm not sure Ward and I have that much in common but we fell in love at first sight.'

'I know it happens,' she says. 'But my family isn't lucky in love. I've had my heart broken once and I don't want it broken again. Plus I've got Tilly to think about. She's still very young but she's old enough to form attachments and I'd hate her to grow attached to Grady if he's not planning on staying around.'

'Relationships are always a risk. We never know whether they'll work or not. But I can understand that it must be more difficult when there's a child involved. And yet Ward was willing to take that risk with me. I fell in love with Eve before I fell in love with him, I think.' I laugh, although there is some truth in that.

'Grady says he thinks Tilly is cute. But that's all he'll say. So I don't want her to spend time with him until I know where things stand with us.'

'So you're going on another date?'

'He said he'll call me.'

'And has he?'

She shakes her head and sips her wine. 'Not yet. But it has been a bit of a weird weekend, hasn't it? I'm hoping he might call me today.'

She glances at her phone which I realise is right beside her plate. He had bloody well better call her. Or he might find himself out of a job.

'I'm starving,' I say, changing the subject. 'Let's eat. And then I'd like to run my Christmas list by you, if that's okay. Aggie and I have agreed it, but I think it's lacking that special something. I discussed it with Tracy earlier, but she didn't come up with any ideas. I'd considered bringing over live reindeer and penguins and several Elves. Actors, not actual Elves. But both Ward and Aggie said no to that.'

'Oh wow! Tilly would've loved to see reindeer and penguins and so would Mum and I. Elves, not so much. Those pointed ears and rosy cheeks remind me of an aunt of mind. The wicked witch of the west, I used to call her, but now that Tilly is old enough to copy everything I say, I have to call her, Aunty Pauline.'

Eleven

Sadly, Natalie couldn't suggest anything extra for my Christmas list, but she did tell me that the Christmas Market on the Harbour Arm in Folkestone has some wonderful stalls selling the most exquisite hand-made Christmas decorations, so I'm now on my way to that and Ward is accompanying me.

That's both good and bad. It means I'm in the water taxi with Grady and I'm cross with him on two counts. One, for telling Nat the things he did, and two for not calling her so far.

But of course, I'd can't tackle him about either, so instead, I make it clear how much I adore Ward, by cuddling him tightly during the crossing and kissing him passionately when I'm certain Grady is looking.

'What was that for?' Ward asks, his eyes dancing with delight. 'Not that I'm complaining. But a kiss like that might make me forget we're on the water taxi and that we have company.'

'It's just because I love you so much and I'm not sure I show it enough lately. We're both always so busy. Me with monitoring the building work, and you with all the other, island stuff.'

'Island stuff?' He laughs, shaking his head. 'Do you actually know what all that "island stuff" entails? I think you should spend every minute of every day with me one week and see for yourself.' He holds me close. 'But I think I'm the one who doesn't show you how much I love you. And I do, Gen. More than you can imagine.'

'I can imagine quite a lot,' I say. 'And I'd love to spend every minute of every day with you and see exactly what you do. I'm not trying to make it sound trivial. I know you do so much and I realise it's complicated and difficult. I just don't know what it involves. But speaking of imagination, I know Aggie and I agreed my Christmas list – and don't get me wrong – I love it, but Tracy, Nat and I all feel it could do with something extra. The ice rink will be great and I'm glad we're keeping the fake polar bears, but I still think the avenue of Nutcrackers lining the stretch of the Boardwalk leading up to Main Road, with each one holding a lantern containing a candle to light the way, would've been lovely.

And they're not alive, they're made of wood. Or hard plastic. I can't recall which. So I don't see what the problem is with those.'

'Fire hazard. And reducing the area of access to the Boardwalk.'

'We could use battery operated candles in the lanterns. And space the Nutcrackers further apart.'

He gives me a thoughtful look and a grin. 'Let me think about it.'

'And I know it would be actors who would perform the Twelve Days of Christmas for everyone on the island to see, and yes, we would need live swans ... and a small pool for them to be 'a-swimming' in, plus the partridge, turtle doves, French hens, calling birds, and geese, would all be alive. And quite how we ensure the geese are 'a-laying' I don't know. But the performance would be a one-off so all the living creatures and the actors would have come and gone in just one day. Don't you think it would be magnificent? And so festive?'

'I do. Yes. But don't you think it would also be noisy, and messy, and chaotic? And can you get a pear tree in winter? Or would that be fake? Now we don't have use of the ferry, it would also be difficult to transport them all to and fro. So I think that is still a definite, no.'

'And the hot air balloon dropping gifts?'

Ward shakes his head. 'Uncertain wind and weather conditions, and not enough open space for it to land in an emergency. You've still got the snow machine, although getting that here may be a problem now.'

'Nope. Jonno and the helicopter can handle that.'

'Oh joy.' Ward is grinning at me. 'I love how enthusiastic you are about making this Christmas special, Gen, but now, with all this additional expense of the pontoons etc., don't you think the streamlined version of your list is the wisest one to go with?'

'And a bit boring.' I pout and he laughs and then kisses me. 'We're here. Let's see what delights we can find at the Christmas Market. We may even get to see some maids a-milking and some Lords a-leaping. Or at least some stall holders serving hot drinks and Christmas shoppers jumping about to keep warm.'

'Can I at least have the pipers piping and the drummers drumming in just a teensy-weensy Christmas procession down Main Road? And maybe an open-topped car made to look like Santa's sleigh?'

'Is the procession still on the list?' He looks surprised as he takes my hand to help me out of the water taxi and nods goodbye to Grady.

'Yes. Even Aggie approved of that.'

I throw Grady a tight smile and ask him if his phone is working.

'Yes,' he says. 'Why?'

'So that we can call you when we want to return to Locke Isle,' I say.

But what I really want to say is, 'Then bloody well call Natalie!'

Ward links my arm in his and we walk towards the Christmas Market. I can already see how wonderful it is but I need to quickly mention one more thing to Ward.

'About the procession. What Aggie actually agreed to is the church choir walking along Main Road, and of Cece and Sylvie handing out freshly baked mini mince pies and shortbread biscuits. I may have added just a couple of other things back in. But please don't be mad. And the pipers and drummers would make it so much better.'

He looks me in the eye and then laughs. 'And with pipes and drums making music you might get your ladies dancing. Okay. Have your pipers and drummers. But just make sure they don't bring anything with feathers along with them. Deal?'

'Deal. And the car and Santa?'

'Fine.' He sighs.

'Oh look, Ward! A carousel!'

'No, Gen! Don't even think about it. We can't have one of those on the island. Perhaps coming here wasn't such a great idea.'

But he's smiling and his eyes are filled with amusement.

I think he's getting as excited about my Christmas list as I am.

Twelve

By the time Ward and I collect Eve from school, we have already sent two lots of shopping back to Locke Isle via Grady and the water taxi. He has deposited all our bags with Roger at the Locke Isle Tourist Office and we will retrieve them later.

Now we are back at the Christmas Market so that Eve can take a ride on the Christmas Carousel. All the horses have wreaths around their necks and the entire Carousel is covered with twinkling lights, as are all the market stalls, shops, and restaurants along the Harbour Arm, in the Marketplace, and The Goods Yard.

It is all so festive and magical that I don't want to leave, and nor does Eve, but it's already dark and although the water taxi has lights and the weather is good today and the sea clam, I can tell Ward wants to get home. It may be more to do with wanting to see what progress has been made on both the pontoon jetty and the other building work than any worries concerning the crossing, but I know he's always aware of how quickly the weather can turn, along this stretch of the English Channel.

'Can't we stay for just one more hour?' Eve asks, eager to experience everything the Christmas Market and Folkestone in general has on offer to celebrate the festive season.

'I think we should get home, honey,' Ward says. 'Don't forget, Grady has to take us and then come all the way back to Folkestone to moor the boat, and then get home to Dover. What about if I promise we'll bring you back here at the weekend?'

'But that's days and days and days away.' She spreads out her hands and arms as if to demonstrate how far away the weekend is and Ward and I both snigger.

'I know. But it'll be here just like that.' Ward snaps his fingers to show how quickly time passes.

He's not wrong. Christmas is getting closer by the minute and I still haven't got everything I need for my Christmas list or my present list. I haven't even written my Christmas cards.

'O-k-a-y,' says Eve, pouting, just like I was earlier.

'This may be a strange question,' I say as we head towards the slipway at the other end of the packed car park, 'but are you sending Christmas cards from you and Eve, or from all three of us, this year? I don't mind either way but I wasn't sure what you had in mind and we need to think about writing them and sending them off fairly soon.'

'Oh.' He looks surprised. 'I had completely forgotten about that. From the four of us. Unless you'd rather send some just from you?'

'No. Erm. Four? Oh, does Horatio send them too? Of course! I remember Eve saying that all three of you get cards from everyone on the island. Do you send special cards? A family photo or something? Or just ordinary Christmas cards?'

'God no! Can you imagine Horatio sitting still long enough for his photo to be taken?'

'He sleeps a lot. We could gather round him then,' I laugh.

'We could. But no. I usually buy Charity Christmas cards. I sign my name, Eve signs hers, and yes, Horatio has his paw dipped in edible ink and stamps his.'

'Really? Or are you kidding?'

He grins at me. 'Nope. Deadly serious.'

'I think we should have casts made of our hands and Horatio's paw and paint them to go on the tree. We would be, figurately speaking, hanging from the branches by our hands. And paw. Wouldn't that be fun?'

'What made you think of that?'

'It just popped into my head.'

'It would be something to keep,' he says. 'We can make them ourselves using flour, salt, and water and baking them in the oven. Eve and I have often made dough ornaments and animals. Hey honey? What do you think of Gen's idea?' He repeats it to Eve and she's so excited she wants to do it right away. 'As soon as we get home,' he says.

'We could make extra and give them away as joke presents. We would, literally, be giving people a hand during the holidays.'

Both Ward and Eve laugh.

'We must give them to Aggie,' Ward says. 'And maybe also to Tracy and Roger.'

'And my dad,' I say. 'It'll be the first joke present he's ever had.'

Thirteen

Ward and I are astonished to see that the pontoon jetty is almost complete. Grady had told us we were in for a surprise but I for one, wasn't sure if he meant good or bad until we pulled up alongside the part that is done and saw how sturdy it is. It's not as long as the former jetty, due to the fact that this is built on the sea and will therefore be subjected to some pretty strong tides and large waves, but the amazing part is, this is fully retractable so that none of it need remain in the water in extreme weather conditions.

Eve is exhausted from all the excitement of the Christmas Market and she's fast asleep on the leather seat in the enclosed cabin of the water taxi. Ward lifts her gently into his arms and she lets out the sweetest snore. If any snore can be classed as sweet that is.

'Look Ward!' Now I'm excited again. 'They've even covered it in wooden decking so that it almost matches the remaining

Boardwalk. How cool is that?'

'Very,' Ward says, looking suitably impressed.

I thought it would sort of bounce when we walked across it, but it feels remarkably similar to the old jetty. Grady helps carry our bags because Ward is carrying Eve.

'I'll take these and your earlier purchases up to Locke Keep,' he says.

'Thanks, Grady,' says Ward.

I simply smile. I'm dying to know if he's called Natalie but obviously I can't ask.

'Several islanders have been down and tried it out,' Grady says, referring to the jetty.

Now's my chance.

'Has my friend Natalie seen it?'

Grady doesn't bat an eyelid.

'Not while I've been here. But she may have seen it when I was crossing, or while I was in Folkestone.'

'I'll call and ask.'

Ward glances at me. 'Why is it so important that Natalie sees it?'

'Because I had lunch with her today and I told her all about it. And I also told her how much I adore you and Eve. And how I've never been happier in my life.'

He furrows his brow, I notice, but most of my attention is focused on Grady, who doesn't react at all.

'That's ... nice,' says Ward, now grinning

at me. 'I hope you tell everyone that.'

'I do,' I say. 'Constantly. Because it's true.'

'Ditto.'

He's looking a tad embarrassed, I assume because we're having this conversation in front of Grady. He doesn't realise this is entirely for Grady's benefit.

So I'm taken completely by surprise when, once we're home and Ward has settled Eve on her bed, he takes my hands in his, and, looking a little nervous, asks me if there's anything I need to tell him concerning Grady.

'What? Why do you ask?'

'Because of the way you've been behaving today,' he says. 'I know you and I have been … snapping at one another a bit lately, but I meant it when I said how much I love you. Please tell me, Gen. And be honest. Do you … do you have feelings for Grady? Or lingering feelings for his brother and you're hoping Grady will tell him about us, and Adam will be jealous?'

I'm so astonished I can't speak and when I see the look of hurt in his eyes and he goes to turn away, I realise this is the second time he's said something about his feelings and I have responded with silence. Although we've told one another we love each other in between, so I'm not sure why he has doubts.

Except that I've been having doubts too, about his love for me.

I tighten my grip on his hands before he can let mine go.

'Look at me, Ward,' I say, and when he does, I beam at him. 'You couldn't be farther from the truth. The only thing I feel towards Grady is irritation over the way he's treating Natalie.'

'Natalie?'

'I'll explain later. As for Adam, he's history. I didn't love him then. I certainly don't love him now. You're the only man for me, Ward. Surely you know that?'

'I … I thought I did. I hoped I was. But … my former wife cheated on me, don't forget, and … you're gorgeous, you're clever, you're rich, you're the woman men dream of, and sometimes I can't believe you've chosen me.'

'I can't believe you've chosen me, Ward! I'm the lucky one here. I think, perhaps, we've both been hurt in the past and we're both feeling a little unsure of ourselves and of each other. We fell in love so fast and yet so deeply that I suppose it's only natural we might have the odd, niggling doubt. Or maybe disbelief that we could be so lucky to find one another. I adore you, Ward. This may sound dramatic, but I would die if you stopped loving me. I've told you that before and I mean it. I think my heart would simply decide there's no point in going on without you.'

He sucks in a breath and the widest smile spreads across his face. 'I feel the same. Except I would go on, because of Eve. But I'd be miserable.'

'Then let's not think about it because if we love one another as much as we say we do – and we do – then neither of us will have to worry about it, will we? Let's give our doubts the boot and trust in our love completely.'

'I can do that.'

He pulls me into his arms and we kiss long and hard and deeply.

'I'm hungry,' a little voice says in the background, and I realise Eve is awake and is staring at us in a sleepy-eyed, not quite with it, fashion.

'Me too,' Ward says in his sexy voice, and I know he doesn't mean for food. 'Sorry, honey.' He moves away from me but throws me the loveliest smile. 'What would you like to eat?'

'Pizza. No. Pancakes. No. Peanut butter sandwiches.'

'So anything beginning with a P then?'

We all laugh at that.

'No. Fish fingers, please,' she says, and grins. 'And peas.'

'I like the sound of that,' I say. 'I'll have the same, please.'

'Fish fingers and peas for three coming right up.'

Horatio barks from the hall. He's been with Aggie all afternoon and she's obviously just brought him back.

'For four,' I say. 'Unless Aggie is staying for supper too. In which case, for five.'

'Five it is.' Ward goes to the freezer and I look for a baking tray. 'What were you saying about Natalie?' he asks, as we prepare supper together.

'She's seeing young Grady,' Aggie says, shrugging off her coat as Horatio comes bounding in and heads directly for Eve.

'Really?' Ward's astounded, and so am I.

'Did Natalie tell you that?' I ask.

'No need. I have eyes. Are we having fish fingers and peas for supper?' She's weaving her way around us, as Eve and Horatio are tumbling on the floor. 'I'm impressed with the pontoons, aren't you? Oh, and Jonas says we might have snow heading our way. I'll help myself to wine.' She leans across me to reach the glasses. 'I assume you both want some too.' She removes the cork and as she empties the bottle into three glasses, says, 'So, did you all enjoy the Christmas Market?'

Sometimes, Aggie leaves me speechless.

And then Ward throws me one of his uber sexy looks that says he's truly happy and content, but would be even more so, if we were alone together right now.

That leaves me both speechless and breathless. And deliriously happy too.

Fourteen

'What is it with me and men?' Natalie asks when I call her the following day.

'He hasn't called yet, I take it?'

'Nope.'

'I was unlucky in love too, until I met Ward, remember? He's out there somewhere, Nat. The man who's meant for you.'

'Well can someone please tell him to get a move on? I love Tilly and Mum but it's been so long since I've ... you know ... and I miss it. Not so much the actual sex part, as the cuddles and companionship. Holding hands, romantic walks, stolen kisses, those tingles you get when he touches you, the looks, the excitement ... the waiting by the phone for the sod to call. Discovering he's buggered off and joined the navy. Sorry. I'm harping back to Tilly's dad. Why do I pick guys connected to the navy? Note to self. Date an astronaut. Or a shepherd.'

'Watching his flock by night?' I laugh.

'At least I would get cheap wool. Think of all the Christmas jumpers, Mum and I could knit.'

'I didn't know you could knit.'

'Can't everyone? Even Tilly has a tiny knitting kit. The needles have rounded ends though.'

'Erm. I can't knit.'

'Really?'

'Not a stitch.'

'I know what to get you for Christmas.'

'Oh, Nat. Please don't get me anything for Christmas. Everything is so expensive. Buy Tilly an extra present instead.'

'I'm going to knit you something. And then give you knitting lessons in the New Year.'

'I'll take the lessons, please. But wool is expensive so don't knit me anything.'

'It isn't if you're dating a shepherd,' she jokes. 'I just need to find one of those.' There's a loud, manly cough in the background. 'Sorry, Gen. I've got to go.'

'That's not Grady is it?' I quickly ask.

'No. But ... it has potential. I'll call you later.'

I spend the next half an hour wondering what she meant by that – and to whom the manly cough belonged. If it wasn't Grady, then there must be someone else on the island whom Nat likes, because she said, "potential" and we'd been discussing dating.

And knitting.

No. She meant a potential date, not a potential Christmas jumper.

Ward calls to tell me that the jetty is as good as complete and the final parts will be added tomorrow.

'What do you think about having a Grand Opening tomorrow afternoon?' he asks.

'Of the jetty? Ooh yes! Any excuse for a celebration. And a new jetty is a good reason for a celebration. I'll order more champagne. And shall I ask Cece and Sylvie to prepare some canapés?'

'We had a can of peas last night,' he quips and I can hear the laughter in his voice.

'Hilarious,' I say. 'And not to quibble, but we had frozen peas last night.'

'Not to quibble even more, but they were boiled.'

'Are we really having a conversation about peas? And to think, people said I'd miss my jet-set lifestyle and all the mega-million pounds business deals. How wrong they were.'

'Ah yes. But this pontoon jetty is your ... *peas* de resistance,' he sniggers.

'You're such a wit. My *pièce de resistance* is going to be my Christmas list.

You wait and see. So, bubbles and nibbles for all the islanders then? Are you sending out a text to all, or shall I spread the word?'

'I'll send a text.'

'Would you mind if I met Natalie for a drink and a bit of pampering at the spa tonight?'

'No. That's fine with me. I'll collect Eve from school, and if you'll be out all evening, I may take her back to the Christmas Market. I'll ask Aggie if she'll have Horatio again for a few hours. She won't mind. She loves that dog. Any news on the Natalie and Grady front?'

'No. But there may be another man waiting in the wings. Hence the spa and drinks. I want to find out what's going on, and to check she's okay.'

'Have fun. But not too much.'

'Ditto,' I say. 'Love you loads.'

'Love you more.'

I let out a swoony sigh after he blows me a kiss down the phone.

I wish Natalie could find a man like Ward. But it took me long enough and she is ten years younger than me. There's still plenty of time.

Are we ever too old to find the one for us, I wonder?

Tracy and Roger found love later in life.

And Bernie, the florist, whose husband

died three years ago, is dating Alfred Shaw, Cece and Sylvie's older brother, whose own wife passed away more than ten years ago. He and Bernie have known one another all their lives and apparently Alfred's had a crush on Bernie for years. Now they're finding love again together and everyone says it won't be long before there's a wedding on Locke Isle. They were on their first date the day I arrived.

But Sylvie made me laugh the other day when I was in White Cliffs Café. She's got a few weird expressions, one being, 'Well paint me green and call me a cucumber.' Ward tells me it means she's cool with something, but I still don't get it.

Anyway, I was there with Tracy and we were discussing love, when Bernie and Alfred came in holding hands.

'Set a date yet?' Cece asked. 'A Christmas engagement would be lovely.'

Bernie tutted and turned redder than the roses she was carrying. No doubt bought from her own shop next door, by Alfred.

'It's too soon to talk like that,' Bernie said, blushing like a teenager.

Alfred looked a little disappointed.

'Too soon?' Sylvie shrieked. 'At the rate you two are going you'll be having your honeymoon in the funeral parlour!'

I know it was in bad taste but I burst out

laughing.

Bernie scowled at me. We didn't get off to a good start the day I arrived, and she hasn't exactly been my biggest fan since, but that's another story.

'I'm only in my ... late sixties,' Bernie said sounding miffed.

To which Sylvie raised her eyebrows. 'Are you counting backwards? You may be ... in your *late* sixties, but Alfred's not. Stop wasting time and make an honest man of him before it's too late.'

'Well really, Sylvie!' Alfred said. 'That's not cricket.'

'We'll do the catering for half price,' said Cece. 'And we'll even throw in a wedding cake if you get married on the same day as you get engaged.'

'Did you say you'll throw a cake at us?' Alfred snapped. 'That's definitely not cricket.'

I'm not sure what happened after that because I had to go and collect Eve from school, but as I said, rumour has it that there will be an engagement and even a wedding before too long, for which, I assume, Bernie will do her own bridal flowers.

I think Cece was joking about the catering. I'm sure they'll do it for free as Alfred is their brother, but if not, I'll suggest to Ward that we pay for it as part of their wedding present. Assuming Bernie intends to invite me. I know she'll invite Ward and Eve, so I'm pretty sure I'll be included, but even if I'm not, I'll still pay for the reception, on behalf of Ward and Eve, and in their names, obviously.

I text Natalie and ask if she's free tonight for a drink and some pampering and she replies that she is. Then I go to see how the boat house, new Boardwalk and helipad are progressing, and after that I pop across to the new jetty and I can't believe how good it looks.

'I know I wasn't keen on your suggestion of a concrete pier, like the Harbour Arm,' Ward says as we stand on the beach and admire the jetty, 'but I can now see that it makes sense. And your proposal to have the pier over near the boathouse is also a good idea. We can still build a new wooden jetty to link to the old original one if we want, and if most of the concrete is covered in wood, like these pontoons are, then you're right. It can still be called the Boardwalk and it won't look like a concrete monstrosity. I've been chatting with several islanders today and apart from one or two, they're all on board.'

'That's fantastic news. We can discuss it with Francis and work can begin next year. I'm about to ask Cece and Sylvie about the can ... snacks for tomorrow. Have you had any response to the invite yet?'

He laughs. 'Only from almost everyone! And there's no need to ask Cece and Sylvie. No sooner had my text gone out than they sent one back saying they'd do the catering for half price. And they'll throw in a Christmas cake and mince pies, too.'

Fifteen

Castle Keep Hotel is a luxury hotel, and also, the only hotel on the island. It's in Frenchman's Cove and has its own section of beach and a heated pool on a small cliff on the opposite side of the island to the jetty.

It's the former Mansion House home of Ward's aunt, and is owned by Ward. After Aggie decided it was too big for her and she wanted something smaller, she moved into Lockekeep Cottage and Ward decided to turn the house into a luxury hotel and Spa.

It's managed by Tristan Goldsby – a rather dashing thirty-five-year-old, who has several 'fans' among the residents of the island and hotel guests, but who pretends he doesn't know. It has a restaurant, a bar, the heated pool, and the Spa.

It's never been fully booked, according to Aggie, but that's partly because its website really needs updating and new, professionally shot photos added to show its true beauty and the spectacular vistas that can be seen from almost every room.

The pool is an infinity pool and is surrounded by scented shrubs and flowers on one side, trees and bushes on another, the hotel itself on another and, of course, the sandy beach and the sea on the last.

The Spa isn't large, but the facilities are first-class and the treatments match many that I've had in eye-wateringly expensive hotels. Here they are exceptionally cheap, all things considered.

I've suggested to Ward that he should increase all the prices, for rooms, the restaurant, and the Spa, but he wants the locals to be able to afford its pleasures. He even has a special 'islanders only day' when everything is sold at cost. It's no wonder he's cash strapped. Or he was until I moved in.

I've opened a joint bank account for us and deposited enough money in it to make the manager of the branch in Folkestone feel he should give us his personal and undivided attention whenever we pop in. I've told Ward several times to consider the money in it, his and mine and to use it whenever and for whatever he wants without having to check with me. But I know he hasn't touched a penny of it, and that makes me cross and a little sad.

'Why won't you use the money in our

account?' I've asked several times.

'Because it's not our money. It's yours.'

'No. It's ours. What's mine is yours and what's yours is mine as far as I'm concerned. Do you think for one moment that if our roles were reversed, I wouldn't be spending that money on all the things I need and want?'

He shrugged at that, and he still does whenever I say it.

'I don't know what you'd do. I only know that it doesn't feel right for me to spend it.'

'That's silly. And rather chauvinistic.'

But nothing's changed.

He's only let me pay for all the building work, and now the pontoons, because he says it's for the benefit of the entire island, but even now he maintains that one day, he'll pay me back.

I don't have the heart to tell him that, unless he drastically changes his ways and stops being so kind and generous to all the islanders it'll take him several hundred years to repay it. I don't want it repaid, so it's irrelevant.

'Oh wow,' Natalie says, when we enter the foyer of Castle Keep Hotel. 'Look at these decorations.'

I am looking at them and I can't believe my eyes. They rival anything that I've seen in the world's finest hotels. And I've stayed in many, if not all, of the most prestigious establishments on the planet.

'Ward led me to believe that a thirty-foot tree was far too tall,' I moan. 'That Christmas tree is at least thirty-three.'

'Good evening, Geneva. Good evening, Natalie. How are we this evening?'

'Hello, Tristan,' I say. 'Surprised.'

'Oh? Anything I can help you with?'

'Yes. How tall is that tree?'

'The Christmas tree? Thirty-four feet, give or take an inch. Is that a problem?'

'Apparently not. Does Ward know it's that tall?'

'Erm.' He looks concerned and unsure of how to respond. 'I believe so. It only went up today. Don't you ... approve? I can have it removed, or ... I'm not sure what's going on. Perhaps you could enlighten me.'

'Hold that thought,' I say.

'Oh dear,' says Natalie.

I take a photo of it on my phone and send it to Ward with a message saying, 'Such a stunningly gorgeous tree. Surely, if it's good enough for Castle Keep Hotel, it's good enough for Locke Keep and the rest of the island? Adding five trees of at least thirty feet, back onto my list. Love you loads. Xx.'

'Sorry, Tristan. It's gorgeous. And not a problem at all. Just a miscommunication. All sorted now. The decorations are beautiful. Who did you hire to do them?'

'Hire? No one. The staff and I did it ourselves.'

'You and the staff did this? All this?' I wave my hand around the foyer.

'Yes,' he says, as if he doesn't understand why I'm shocked.

There are massive oversized baubles tied with the most elegant of bows. There are silver bells, wreaths, garlands, and flowers. The tree is threaded through with exquisite gold ribbon and has several hundred white lights, and red and gold baubles, decorations, and ornaments all displayed to perfection.

'Then, if you can spare the time, I wonder if you and your staff could come and help me put up some decorations around the island and in Locke Keep. I'll pay you all, of course. Handsomely.'

'Erm. I'd be happy to, Geneva. I'm sure we all would. But I'm not sure I understand. The thing is. Everyone on Locke Isle tends to put up their own decorations. The lights on Main Road stay up all year, although unlit apart from at Christmas. Are you saying that Ward intends to make changes this year?'

'Oh!' I look at Natalie, who shrugs. 'Erm. I'd discussed it with Aggie, and Ward too, and yes, I … I thought we would be. Perhaps I need to check again. Let's go and get a drink, Nat? Thanks, Tristan. I'll see you later.'

'Let's,' she says.

'Of course,' says Tristan. 'Let me know if and when you need me to help you. Enjoy your evening.'

I stop and turn back to look at him.

'Just one other thing. Where did you get that tree?'

His brows furrow as if he's being tested. 'We cut it down, as we do each year.'

'Cut it down? From where?'

'From the copse at Locke Keep.'

'The copse at Locke Keep? I see. Thank you. It really is a beautiful tree.'

Natalie grins at me. 'You didn't know there was a copse at Locke Keep, did you? Or that there are Christmas trees on the island. Well, pine trees. They're only Christmas trees once they're cut down and dressed.'

'Did you know?'

She shrugs. 'I've lived here all my life, so yes. There's always a tree at the foot of the steps of Locke Keep, but it's not as big as the one here.'

'Why didn't you tell me this before?'

'Sorry. You didn't ask. You just told me what was on your list. I assumed you knew about the trees. But I can see why Ward thinks five is too many. The copse isn't large and there aren't a lot of trees. Certainly not big trees.'

'I was going to have them shipped in. Why didn't he tell me about the copse?'

Natalie sniggers. 'Erm. You can see it from the windows of Locke Keep, Gen. And you walk past it every day. How have you *not* seen it?'

'The trees around the keep, you mean?'

She nods. 'Yes.'

'There are pine trees?'

She nods again.

'I … I've never noticed them.'

She shakes her head. 'I hate to say this, but I think you're so used to designer labels on everything you buy that unless a tree is labelled, "Christmas tree" you wouldn't think it was one.'

'That's a bit harsh,' I laugh. 'But actually, you're probably not far from the truth. I think I'd better open my eyes and really take notice of what's around me.'

A message beeps through from Ward. 'I haven't seen it in real life yet. It does look gorgeous. Will agree to three trees. Five is too many. Talk later. Have fun. I adore you. Xx'

'Yeah right. I need that drink, Nat. Let's forget about trees. I want to hear about this … person who had potential today. Who is he and did anything happen?'

She grins and blushes, but waits until we're sitting at a table in a cosy corner of the bar, right beside the roaring log fire and the beautifully decorated mantelpiece.

'His name is Felix and he's one of the workforce for the Boardwalk. I've seen him a few times since they arrived. He even walked me home one day last week. But he's not handsome, like Grady. And he's never asked me out or shown any interest in me really. He did play catch with Tilly a few weeks ago and he said his sister has children around the same age as Tilly. He's young though. Around my age, I think. And I thought he had a girlfriend, but I heard this morning that he hasn't. Mum popped in a little while before you called, and told me that she was chatting to one of the women on his team. I think that means that Mum probably asked outright, because when Felix walked me home, Mum saw him. Anyway, the woman said Felix is single and that she happens to know he likes me. Mum told me that, but I didn't think anything of it. Mum's always trying to set me up. She even tried to get Tristan to go out with me. Can you believe that?'

'Tristan's handsome. And he's lovely.'

'Yes. And ten years older than me.'

'I'm ten years older than you!'

'I'm not dating you, Gen. You're a friend.'

'Really? And there's me thinking we had something special.' I pout stupidly and sigh dramatically.

'Behave!' she says, nudging my arm. 'So where was I? Oh yes. When you and I were chatting, Felix came into the shop with a bunch of yellow roses and I could tell by the way he was looking at me that he might be about to ask me out.'

'Oh, Nat! That's fantastic. And did he?'

She nods and smiles. 'He did.'

'And you said yes?'

'I said I might.'

'Natalie!'

'Grady might call. I'm a one man, woman.'

'Grady should've called right away. You're too good for him. I like the sound of this Felix. Don't you like him?'

'I like him. Yes. Does he make my heart flutter? No. Although ... it did sort of sit up and take notice when he gave me the flowers and our fingers touched for a second. There was a little tingle. But then I realised I'd got a thorn sticking in my finger. At least he helped me get it out.'

'Oh Natalie! He sounds really nice. Please give him a chance.'

'I'm giving Grady one more day. If he doesn't call by tomorrow, he's history.'

'It's the Grand Opening of the pontoon jetty tomorrow. Grady will be there.'

She sits upright and breathes in deeply. 'I really hope he calls. Or that he asks me out again at the Grand Opening.'

I rather hope he doesn't, because I think Felix is probably nicer, judging by the way they've both behaved so far.

But it's her life, not mine so I mustn't interfere.

Sixteen

'I don't know what to do,' Natalie says, after asking to have a quick word with me at the Grand Opening of the jetty. 'So I need your advice.'

'Okay. I'll try to help if I can. What's happened? I saw you speaking with a lovely man who I assume is Felix, and I also saw you chatting with Grady, so I'm guessing this has something to do with them.'

'Yes,' she says. 'I said I'd give Grady until today to call. Well he didn't. And when Mum, and me, and Tilly first arrived here, it looked as if he was actually trying to avoid me. Then Felix came over and started chatting. He does look nice today, doesn't he? He and his colleagues have got a bit dressed up for the occasion. I've only seen him in his work clothes until today and I'm surprised how different he looks. Anyway, when Felix went to get some drinks, Grady asked to talk to me. He said he's been rushed off his feet and that there's a bit of an issue at home and that's why he hasn't called. He asked who Felix was and seemed a little jealous when I told him that Felix has sked me out. Grady said he wants to see me again and he hopes I won't do anything foolish, like go out with another man. What do I do, Gen? I think I like them both.'

'Then tell Grady you want to go out on a second date with him, but that you want to go on a date with Felix, too, and that you're not going to do anything, 'foolish' with either of them. Whatever he may mean by 'foolish'. If it was me, though, I think I'd be leaning towards Felix. I'm not sure what this issue is at home but Grady hasn't said anything to Ward or to me about an issue.'

'You think he's making it up?'

'I think it's odd that he doesn't call when he said he would, and that he can attend this event even though there's an issue at home, and yet he doesn't come straight up to you and explain about why he hasn't called. It's only when he sees you with someone else that he comes and tells you this.'

'Yes. I see. Erm. I need to think about it, don't I?'

'What does your mum think?'

'She likes Felix. She thinks Grady's got a very high opinion of himself. But he's got good reason to have, hasn't he?'

'Yes. But everyone should have a high opinion of themselves. If we don't think highly of ourselves, why should anyone else think highly of us? I don't mean we should be arrogant. I mean we should all believe we're as good as the next person.'

'You'd date Felix though?'

'Yes. But I haven't met him so I'm simply going by his behaviour towards you and Tilly. You said yourself that he played with her. Has Grady done that?'

She shakes her head. 'No.'

'Then see if he will tonight. If not, I'd say you might be better off with Felix. But only you can make this decision, Nat.'

'Yeah. You're right. Thanks, Gen. Oh? What happened about the trees?'

I grin at her and glance over at Ward who is chatting with Felix right now.

'Ward showed me the trees, and today we went to the hotel and he saw the one there and how stunning it is. We're having one big tree outside, and Ward is asking Tristan and the hotel staff to decorate it, because as much as I love the idea of doing it, I'm not sure I'd be any good. But we're also having one in Locke Keep and Ward, Eve and I are going to decorate that.'

'So it all worked out then?'

'Sort of. Yes. Let me know how it goes with your men,' I say. 'And follow your heart and your head if you can.'

'Is that what you did with Ward?'

'No. I just fell head over heels in love with him.'

'I want what you have,' she sighs. 'Only not with Ward. No offence meant by that.'

'None taken. Good luck, Nat. I'm here if you need me.'

As soon as Natalie goes back to her mum and Tilly, Ward saunters over to me.

'I've just been talking with Felix. Personally, I think he's a better match for Nat than Grady will ever be.'

'I've just told her something similar.' I'd told Ward about it last night and he'd told me not to get involved.

'What happened to not getting involved?'

'That was your suggestion. I didn't agree to it. A bit like you didn't agree to me having five trees.' I smile at him.

'As I told you last night, if you really want five trees, have them. But you'll have to buy some because we don't have enough on the island to cut down that many at once.'

'So you're not against me having the trees? You just don't want me to have yours?'

'You can have anything of mine you want, Gen. Anything. Just not five trees at once. Unless you're willing to plant several more and buy trees every year until the new ones are fully grown. I'm not sure why we're arguing about this. I think five trees is excessive. You'd agreed with me and Aggie. But it's up to you, Gen. I don't want to fight with you about trees. Especially when we wouldn't have this wonderful jetty if not for you. So have fifty-five trees if it'll make you happy. But not cut down from the ones here, please, that's all I ask.'

'Fine. Fifty-five it is then. I'll have them shipped in from Norway.'

He does a double take and then he laughs. 'I love you, Gen. That was a joke though, wasn't it?'

'Yes.'

'Right. I need to go. I've got a little surprise for you. I really hope you like it.'

'What sort of surprise?'

'It's something from your Christmas list. Sort of.'

He waves at me and rushes off and I return to Eve, Horatio, and Aggie. Tracy and Roger come to join us and we chat and drink and eat, and then a shout goes up and someone points out to sea.

We all turn round and there's the water taxi approaching. It's got a little Christmas tree on its bow, and it's lit up, and there's a row of fairy lights running along both sides and another little tree in the cabin.

Music is in the air and as I look around I

see the church choir, all dressed as Elves, approaching. They're singing the Carol of the Bells, my all-time favourite, as Ward knows. And each one of them is carrying a lantern with a candle – battery-operated I assume.

And then another shriek goes up and just as the water taxi pulls up alongside the new pontoon jetty, the ferry appears and that too has a Christmas tree but it's on the main deck and it's also decorated with lights, as is the ferry.

Tears prick at my eyes as I watch Ward manoeuvre it into position beside the jetty and once both boats are safely moored, Grady and Ward strut along the jetty towards the huge cheering crowd.

Every islander must be here tonight and the atmosphere is like a Christmas party. People are singing along with the choir, as are several dogs, including Horatio. Eve, Aggie and I join in too, but as Ward closes the distance between us and the choir sings its final note, Ward asks for silence, and the heaving crowd obliges.

'We're only here today because of the kindness, generosity, and sheer brilliance of one person, and all the people who have worked so hard and so fast to make her vision a reality. So let's thank her and everyone involved and show her how much she means to us all. Geneva McBriar, I want you to know that this island wouldn't be the same without you. Not for me. Not for any of us.'

'No,' someone shouts out from the crowd. 'It'd be a lot quieter!' And then he roars with laughter and I can see it's Jonas Barnaby. 'We love you, Geneva. You're one of us now, whether you like it or not.'

'To Geneva!' Ward says, raising a glass that someone has handed him.

'Geneva!' Everyone shouts at once.

Now tears are streaming down my face, and then I see Dad and I gasp in astonishment. He's smiling and he looks like the epitome of a proud father.

'Come and say a few words, Gen,' Ward says.

I wipe the tears away and stumble towards Ward.

'I can't believe you've done this,' I say. 'I'm going to kill you later.'

He laughs. 'I thought you might.'

I turn and face the crowd and I see Bernie and she's smiling at me. If she likes me now, life is good.

'Erm. I don't know what to say. I love this island. I love Ward, and Eve and Horatio. And Aggie.'

'Nice to know I come after the dog,' Aggie laughs.

'And Tracy and Roger. And Natalie.'

'Are you going to name everyone on the

island?' Jonas jokes.

'Not you, Jonas,' I say, laughing. 'I'm not prepared for this. I didn't expect it.'

'Sounds like an Oscar speech to me,' says Sylvie.

'Do I get a statuette too?' I ask.

'No. But you do get cake,' Cece says.

'Then I'll just say, thank you. Thank you for allowing me to be part of this wonderful community. Thank you for putting up with the noise and dust and dirt and disruption and for having faith in this project. It'll be fabulous when it's done, and we can look forward to welcoming more people to the island. But it's really Ward you should be thanking, not me. He's the one who wants you all to have the lives he believes you all deserve. To have your own businesses and own your own homes. To make a good living and be happy, safe, and secure in the knowledge that no one can ever take any of this away from you. Let's say a huge thank you to Ward for being the wonderful man that he is. I'm proud and honoured to be his girlfriend and his partner. To Ward Locke, everyone!'

'To Ward!' they all cheer, and Ward looks terribly embarrassed but also extremely happy as he beams at me.

'Oh, and to Captain Eve and first mate Horatio who, along with Ward, bring me so much joy. Far more than I ever thought possible.'

'To Eve and Horatio!' the crowd cheers.

'And to my dad.' I raise my glass to him and he looks astonished. 'For making me who I am, and for being here when we all really needed him. To Dad.'

'To Dad!' everyone shouts and then they all laugh, because most of them have no idea who 'Dad' is.

'And that's enough speeches. Let's drink and be merry. It'll soon be Christmas.'

'Amen to that,' shouts Aggie.

The choir bursts into song and I turn to Ward and we smile at one another.

'How and when, did you do all this?' I ask.

'I happen to have a Christmas list of my own,' he says and then he kisses me.

I don't think even live reindeer and penguins could top this.

I've never been so happy in my life.

Seventeen

Dad doesn't stay, and Jonno flies him back to the mainland less than half an hour after the speeches. But Rome wasn't built in a day, and Dad does come and tell me how proud he is of me before he leaves.

'You're not following the path I would've chosen for you, Geneva, but then, you never did. I was hoping your mum might be here, but you know her. I'm proud to call you my daughter. We may not agree on some things, but we can agree on this. You're one hell of a woman, Geneva McBriar. I'll see you soon. Enjoy the party.'

And then, after saying goodbye to Ward, he leaves.

The party continues until late, but Ward and Grady return the water taxi and the ferry to the mainland to moor overnight. Until the boathouse is built, we still can't really keep them here. Jonno flies them both back to Locke Isle and he stays too.

I drink far too much for my own good but I wake the next day without a hangover, so I can't have drunk as much as I thought.

'The snow machine is arriving today,' I say, tugging the duvet from Ward.

He groans and tugs it back. He did drink quite a lot, I think, but not until after Jonno brought him and Grady back to the island.

I text Jonno to see what time we're expecting the snow machine. It's coming in several parts and he is flying it here by helicopter, and a cargo net and cables. There's a specialist team coming over on the ferry to fix it together.

And naturally, as it is sod's law, it actually starts snowing.

Before long it's turned into a blizzard and no one is going anywhere today, including Jonno … and the snow machine.

Eve, of course is thrilled and wants to build snowmen and have snowball fights. Horatio isn't quite as keen and keeps disappearing back to his lovely warm bed.

As the workforce on site can't do much in heavy snow, they too join in and before long, it's an all-out war, although a friendly one, between the workforce and the islanders.

The islanders, with Ward as our leader, win, and the losers all buy the drinks.

Which means Ward wakes up with a

hangover the following day, as do I and quite a few others.

Natalie has gone out on her second date with Grady, who pulled out all the stops, and bought her expensive flowers, expensive perfume, and expensive wine, and the most expensive items on the menu at Castle keep Hotel.

He'd also booked a room for the night and whether he hoped she'd share it with him or not, I don't know, but she didn't.

'He's gorgeous,' she says, when I ask her about it. 'But he pointed out that everything was the best, as if he thought I might not have realised how much it was costing. I felt as if I was being bought, and I didn't like that feeling.'

'I can understand that,' I say, thinking what a jerk he was being.

'And when he said he'd booked a room, I wanted to run, not walk away. I told him I had to get home to Tilly and when he asked why my mum couldn't take care of 'the kid' for one night, I did get up and say I had to go. He wasn't happy, but I think I've dodged a bullet.'

I do too. Especially when Ward tells me the next day that he found Grady's draft manuscript on the ferry, and although he probably shouldn't have, he read some of it.

'It's about a single mum with jet black

hair, who lives with her mum, works in a shop, and has a child aged four. Basically, it's Natalie's life story and I think I need to tell him it's not going to happen. He's a great captain, but I don't think this will work out.'

I'm horrified, of course, and agree. Which means we'll be looking for a new ferry captain. In the meantime, Ward, and occasionally, Roger will be back at the helm.

The snow doesn't last and work is progressing well on the Boardwalk once again.

The snow machine arrives and is set up, so we now have the best of both worlds. Snow, but only when and where we want it. Eve wants it right outside our door, and as often as possible. Ward wants it as far away as possible, and I want it where everyone can enjoy it, so we reach a compromise.

The closer we get to Christmas, the more I realise that Ward was right all along.

It's not about how much money you spend. It's about sharing the joy with others and creating memories together.

After the Grand Opening of the jetty there seems to have been a slight shift. Everyone seems more settled, somehow, including Ward and me. We no longer question our love for one another, or doubt what he other is planning. Ward has even spent some money from our joint bank account, although only for some lights to decorate the Boardwalk and the jetty, but it's a start.

Bernie and Alfred have today announced their engagement, but no wedding date has been set as yet. There's going to be a huge party at the weekend and yes, I've been invited.

My five trees have arrived. Yes. I ordered all five, and all of them have been decorated by Tristan and the staff of Castle Keep Hotel. There's one outside at the foot of the steps, one at each end of the island, one on Main Street, and one on the jetty, but on the beach end, not the seaward end.

Ward, Eve, Aggie and I, decorated the one other tree that was cut from the copse, and that's the tree in Locke Keep. It isn't thirty feet. I compromised on that. It's sixteen and that's plenty.

And Ward, Eve and I did plant several new trees to take its place in the hope we'll have trees for Locke Keep for many years to come.

The days are flying and it's almost Christmas Eve. Ward and I have been invited to a thing called The Mistletoe Dance at Betancourt, in Betancourt Bay. We can see the stately home of Betancourt from here and it's beautiful. We can also see part of the village and that's pretty too. The eldest son is a friend of Ward's but I haven't met him yet. His name is Grifforde, but everyone calls him Griff.

'He works and lives in London most of the time, so I don't see him much myself,' Ward says. 'The Mistletoe Dance has been held for hundreds of years, but I've only been a few times, and since Eve was born, never. I know how quickly the weather can change and although she's eight now and I could leave her with Aggie, or Tracy and Roger, I would never forgive myself if I got stuck on the mainland on Christmas Eve and couldn't get home to be here on Christmas Day. No dance is more important than that.'

'We could have our own dance here,' I suggest. 'In the Great Hall.'

'We could.' He looks as if he likes the idea. 'But I wouldn't want Griff to think we were competing. Although their dance is mainly for the residents of the village, many prominent business people and celebrities are invited.'

'Then let's make ours strictly for the residents of Locke Isle and no one else. Oh, except family, so Dad can be invited. Could we do that next year, perhaps?'

Ward smiles at me and hugs me close. 'We could. I expect you'll want to make a list.'

'I'll start one right now. We'll need trees and reindeer and penguins and...' I laugh.

Storms blow in the next day, but they only hit the Channel and not the mainland. It's so frustrating to look across a body of raging water from an island being lashed with rain and battered by winds and see the sun shining over Folkestone. But I've been on a street once where it was pouring with rain on one side of the road and bone dry on the other.

The ferry can't sail and nor can the water taxi and even the helicopter couldn't make the trip in this weather, although as that's now back in Edinburgh we don't have access to it anyway. Dad says we can borrow it whenever we want, but for now, we're all trapped on the island. And yet, no one, feels trapped, including me and we have all we need. Apart from Eve's main present of that pirate ship. I hope the storms clear before Christmas Eve.

The pontoon jetty has been retracted from the water but the waves are crashing on the shore and it's a tense time. The rest of the old Boardwalk holds out, and although work has now ceased for the Christmas break, the site and everything there stays safe and sound, so that's one less thing to worry about.

And Felix, who is now dating Natalie, is also stuck on the island. He decided to stay on for a few days but was meant to return to the mainland to be with his family, and then the storms hit.

We had been expecting them but hoped they wouldn't last as long as they have.

Ward offered him a free room in the hotel, but Sharon, Natalie's mum offered him a bed at Croft Cottage the home she shares with Natalie and Tilly, and to his credit, he opted to stay there and not live a life of luxury at Castle Keep Hotel. Grady would've chosen the hotel.

We haven't seen Grady due to the storms, but Ward has already told him that he doesn't think things will work out, and Grady didn't seem surprised.

Felix has been fixing up a few things in and around Croft Cottage that needed some work, so he's been a true gem. It's pretty clear that he is falling in love with both Natalie and Tilly, and he gets on well with Sharon. I don't think it'll be long until he moves here on a permanent basis. He'll be working at the beach site for months to come, so nothing has to be decided on that score for a while.

We have been attending carol services at the church of St Mary on the Water, the only church on the island. The Reverend Minton Bloom is in his seventies and hard of hearing so he shouts at the top of his voice, and has the funniest conversations because he refuses to wear a hearing aid.

The procession down Main Road has been cancelled along with the pipers and drummers and Santa's car. I'm disappointed but it goes to show that no matter how much money one has, good weather can't be bought.

'Unless we spend next Christmas in the Caribbean,' I joke.

'No chance,' Ward says. 'I adore you, Gen, but Christmases should be cold, so I'm not going anywhere at Christmas.'

'Not even to Dad's ski chalet in Aspen?'

'Hmm. I might go there. But not for Christmas, no. Unless you really want to. I've spent every Christmas here my entire life and it may be selfish but I can't imagine spending Christmas anywhere other than on Locke Isle.'

Oddly enough, nor can I.

Eighteen

'Well,' I say, staring out at a sunny Folkestone yet again as more rain and wind batters the island on Christmas Eve morning. 'It looks as if we're all set for a stormy Christmas and a disappointed child – and that's just me! I dread to think how Eve will feel.'

Ward laughs. 'She won't mind, and neither will you, because the main thing is we're together and we're warm and dry and we have all that we need for a lovely Christmas.'

And to prove him right, Eve dances out of her room with Horatio close behind her.

'This Christmas is going to be the best Christmas yet!' she announces.

'Is it?' I'm not convinced.

I was hoping it would be and if I'd had everything on my list I think it could've been, but although Ward is right and we have each other and a roof over our heads and food on the table and a fire in the heath, all of the presents I'd ordered for Eve and for Ward, and for Aggie, and for Natalie, Tilly and Sharon, and for Tracy and Roger, and everyone else on the island, haven't arrived.

And they won't come now.

Unless there really is a Father Christmas and he can weather a storm over Locke Isle – and we all know that isn't going to happen.

'Yes,' says Eve. 'And do you know why?'

'No,' I say. 'Why?'

She jumps onto my lap and hugs me and then she pulls Ward close and hugs him. And never one to be left out, Horatio jumps on us, and we all hug him.

'Because,' she says, beaming at Ward and me, 'we're a family. A dad, a mum, a daughter, and a dog. And because we love each other very, very much.'

'We do,' I say, feeling choked that she has referred to me as a mum. Her mum.

And I can see from the way Ward is looking at me that he's pleased about that too.

'We are,' he says, and then he twists around and looks me in the eye. 'And do you know what would make it even better?'

'No,' Eve and I say in unison.

He shifts Eve and Horatio to one side, pulls out something from his pocket, and gets down on one knee. 'If we make it official.

Geneva McBriar, I couldn't love you more if I tried. Will you please say you'll be my wife, and Eve's mum, and Horatio's mum too. Will you marry me, Geneva?'

I'm speechless again, but this time only for a second as Eve gasps with delight and claps her hands, and Horatio barks and does a funny little dance. And then I throw myself into Ward's arms and say, 'Yes! Yes! Yes!'

Eve is right. This is going to be the best Christmas ever. And it's not because of expensive gifts, or parades, or trees, or Elves, or ice rinks, or even snow machines. It's because we love each other and we're a family.

Nineteen

I must confess though, I am delighted when, an hour or so later, just as we're gathering Aggie, and Nat and her family and Felix, and Tracy and Roger together to tell them the good news, the rain stops, the wind dies down and blows away, and the sun appears over Locke Isle.

And later, as we're all drinking champagne and toasting Christmas Eve, a strange sound fills the air.

The whirring grows louder and we all rush to the windows and look out. I can't believe my eyes and I don't think anyone else can either.

'Is that what I think it is?' Ward asks, incredulous.

'Bloody hell!' says Aggie.

There are not one, but two helicopters approaching Locke Isle.

One has a large red bow wrapped around the sides; the other has cables and a cargo net and is carrying something beneath it.

'A pirate ship!' Eve shrieks. 'And it's flying!'

'Pirate ships only fly on Christmas Eve,' Ward says, obviously concerned that she might be disappointed when it doesn't any other day.

'Like reindeer?' she says, her eyes sparkling, her cheeks flushed, and the widest smile I've ever seen on her face.

'Just like reindeer,' I say.

'Who's the helicopter for?' Eve asks. 'I'm too young to fly.'

And that's when I spot my dad.

'I think that might be for me,' I say, looking at Ward who is clearly as astonished as me, as Dad flies past and heads towards the roof of the boathouse.

'I'd better go and help that thing land,' Felix says.

I assume he's referring to the pirate ship not the helicopters.

'I'll come too,' says Ward.

'I think we'd all better go,' says Sharon.

As we head towards the beach, the entire island appears to have come out and it's all hands on deck, both figuratively and literally speaking

The pirate ship lands safely in the water right beside the now extended again, pontoon jetty, and Eve can't wait to climb aboard.

Dad lands the other helicopter and saunters over to join us, and then Jonno lands beside that one and he joins us too.

'You'll be needing these,' Dad says, handing me the keys to the helicopter wrapped in ribbon. 'And I've thrown in flying lessons for you and Ward. No point in having one if you don't know how to fly it. I hope it's okay that I didn't call first. I wasn't sure we'd make it with the bad weather.'

'You're most welcome,' says Ward.

'And congratulations to you both,' Dad says. 'We've brought champagne.'

'How ... how did you know, Dad? I was going to call and tell you later.'

'Ward called and asked for my permission,' Dad says, smiling at him.

'You're engaged?' Sylvie shrieks. 'Congratulations! This calls for a party. And cake.'

And before we know it, everyone is on the beach drinking and dancing and singing.

'I see we seem to have acquired McBriar Airlines,' Ward says, grinning.

'Locke Isle Scenic Flights,' I correct.

'And Pirates of Locke Isle,' says Eve. 'See. Best Christmas yet.'

'Best Christmas ever,' says Ward.

'Best Christmas so far,' I say. 'We've got many more to come.'

'Yes we have,' Ward says, pulling me into his arms. 'And a wedding. And that's the thing I'll be looking forward to the most. Merry Christmas my darling, Gen.'

'Merry Christmas, my darling, Ward. I'd better make a list for our wedding, don't you think? Tell me. Can reindeers pull carriages?'

Ward roars with laughter and then he kisses me and this really is the best Christmas I've ever had.

So far.

Coming soon

Visit www.emilyharvale.com to see what's coming next.

Plus, sign up for Emily's newsletter, or join her Facebook group, for all the latest news about her books.

Stay in touch with

Emily Harvale

If you want to be the first to hear Emily's news, find out about book releases, see covers and maybe chat with other fans, there are a few options for you:

Visit: www.emilyharvale.com

and subscribe to Emily's newsletter via the 'sign me up' box. Or, if you really love Emily's books, apply to join Emily's Open House here:

www.emilyharvale.com/MembersClub

Or ask to join Emily's exclusive Facebook Group here:

www.emilyharvale.com/FacebookGroup

Alternatively, just come and say 'Hello' on social media:

@EmilyHarvaleWriter

@EmilyHarvale

@EmilyHarvale

A Note from Emily

Thank you for reading this book. I really hope it brought a smile to your face. If so, I'd love it if you'd leave a short review on Amazon, or even just a rating. And, maybe, tell your friends, or mention it on social media.

A little piece of my heart goes into all my books. I can't wait to bring you more stories that I hope will capture your heart, mind and imagination, allowing you to escape into a world of romance in some enticingly beautiful settings.

To see my books, or to sign up for my newsletter, please visit my website. The link is on the previous page.

I love chatting to readers, so pop over to Facebook or Instagram and say, 'Hello'. Or better yet, there's my lovely Facebook group for the latest book news, chats and general book-related fun. Again, you'll find details on the previous page.

Also by Emily Harvale

The Golf Widows' Club
Sailing Solo
Carole Singer's Christmas
Christmas Wishes
A Slippery Slope
The Perfect Christmas Plan
Be Mine
It Takes Two
Bells and Bows on Mistletoe Row

Lizzie Marshall series:
Highland Fling – book 1
Lizzie Marshall's Wedding – book 2

Goldebury Bay series:
Ninety Days of Summer – book 1
Ninety Steps to Summerhill – book 2
Ninety Days to Christmas – book 3

Hideaway Down series:
A Christmas Hideaway – book 1
Catch A Falling Star – book 2
Walking on Sunshine – book 3
Dancing in the Rain – book 4

Hall's Cross series
Deck the Halls – book 1
The Starlight Ball – book 2

Michaelmas Bay series
Christmas Secrets in Snowflake Cove – book 1
Blame it on the Moonlight – book 2

Lily Pond Lane series
The Cottage on Lily Pond Lane – four-part serial
Part One – New beginnings
Part Two – Summer secrets
Part Three – Autumn leaves
Part Four – Trick or treat
Christmas on Lily Pond Lane
Return to Lily Pond Lane
A Wedding on Lily Pond Lane
Secret Wishes and Summer Kisses on Lily Pond Lane

Wyntersleap series
Christmas at Wynter House – Book 1
New Beginnings at Wynter House – Book 2
A Wedding at Wynter House – Book 3
Love is in the Air – spin off

Merriment Bay series
Coming Home to Merriment Bay – Book 1
(four-part serial)
Part One – A Reunion
Part Two – Sparks Fly
Part Three – Christmas
Part Four – Starry Skies
Chasing Moonbeams in Merriment Bay – Book 2
Wedding Bells in Merriment Bay – Book 3

Seahorse Harbour series
Summer at my Sister's – book 1
Christmas at Aunt Elsie's – book 2
Just for Christmas – book 3
Tasty Treats at Seahorse Bites Café – book 4
Dreams and Schemes at The Seahorse Inn – book 5
Weddings and Reunions in Seahorse Harbour – book 6

Clementine Cove series
Christmas at Clementine Cove – book 1
Broken Hearts and Fresh Starts at Cove Café – book 2

Friendships Blossom in Clementine Cove – book 3

Norman Landing series
Saving Christmas – book 1
A not so secret Winter Wedding – book 2
Sunsets and Surprises at Seascape Café – book 3
A Date at the end of The Pier – book 4

Locke Isle series
A Summer Escape – book 1
Christmas on Locke Isle – book 2

Betancourt Bay series
That Mistletoe Moment – book 1
That Winter Night – book 2

To see a complete list of my books, or to sign up for my newsletter, go to www.emilyharvale.com/books

There's also an exclusive Facebook group for fans of my books. www.emilyharvale.com/FacebookGroup

Or scan the QR code below to see all my books on Amazon.

Printed in Great Britain
by Amazon

38695231R00101